McKendree

McKendree

DOUGLAS HIRT

A DOUBLE D WESTERN

DOUBLEDAY

New York London Toronto Sydney Auckland

A Double D Western
PUBLISHED BY DOUBLEDAY
a division of Bantam Doubleday Dell Publishing Group, Inc.
666 Fifth Avenue, New York, New York 10103

Double D Western, Doubleday,
and the portrayal of the letters DD
are trademarks of Doubleday, a division of
Bantam Doubleday Dell Publishing Group, Inc.

Library of Congress Cataloging-in-Publication Data

Hirt, Douglas.
McKendree / Douglas Hirt.—1st ed.
    p.   cm.—(A Double D western)
I. Title.
PS3558.I727M34   1992
813'.54—dc20   91-46431
CIP

ISBN 0-385-41396-3
Printed in the United States of America
August 1992
First Edition

10 9 8 7 6 5 4 3 2 1

To Ed and Mildred Hirt—
this one is for you.

The Thick Timber

ONE

JOSIAH McKENDREE caught the look Charles Goodwin gave him, and the imperceptible nod of his head as he stepped out the door. McKendree pushed back from the table, taking his wide-brimmed beaver hat in hand. "I'm going outside for a breath, Noreen," he said, glancing at his wife then briefly at Rachael Goodwin as he squeezed around the table in the tidy two-room cabin.

"Now don't you and Charles go running off somewhere, Josh," Noreen said. "We'll be needing to get home before dark."

"I'll be out front," McKendree said, ducking under the low door into the slanting afternoon sunlight. The air outside was heavy as a wet towel, and not much better than it had been inside the little two-room house he'd helped the Goodwins build almost ten years before.

On the porch Charles Goodwin stopped by the railing to lean a shoulder against a peeled upright. The shade of an ancient oak kept the early September heat at bay. He batted at the swarm of gnats that moved like a black veil in front of his eyes and glanced up the cart track where Lucas, Sarah and Tommy were chasing a rusty wheel rim with a forked stick. Their laughter rang among the trees like a crisp new bell, mixing with the happy grunting of the two yellow dogs that bounded alongside them.

McKendree packed his clay pipe and put a match to it. "Something on your mind, Charles?" he said, watching his friend watching the children play. A cardinal swooped through the clearing where the cabin stood and a pair of gray squirrels chased each other around the bole of the oak tree. Charles didn't answer at once.

McKendree puffed out a gray cloud that kept the gnats at a comfortable distance. Overhead a hawk shrieked and dove toward the tawny corn, beyond the rail fence, that McKendree had helped Goodwin plant that spring. His own field needed picking soon, and the potato-planted hillside would need digging too. There were pressing chores to be done now that fall was around the corner. He had to lay in a stack of wood soon, but more immediate, there was that ride into St. Elizabeth tomorrow.

Inside the cabin Rachael laughed. A fly buzzed in the still, hot air. Lilly, the Goodwins' nursing hound, barked. Then Charles pushed away from the post and turned a concerned face at McKendree. He was a husky man, a good six inches shorter than McKendree, with a square jaw, strong shoulders and powerful arms that could wrestle a plow all day long without tiring. He was not a man to allow trifles to worry him. McKendree's neck began to itch back behind his right ear—a need for caution always made itself known there first.

"What is it?" he asked with a growing concern.

Goodwin nodded his head at the children playing in the yard. "Sarah will be fifteen in another couple months. She's growing into a fine-looking gal, like her ma." He paused to watch his daughter with unbridled affection shining in his brown eyes. "You know, Josh, Rachael wasn't much older than Sarah is now when I met her. I was twenty-six, and I figured she was about the prettiest thing that ever did come my way."

"Rachael still turns a man's head, Charles," McKendree said, knowing he was taking the long way around to the heart of the matter. He eased his weight onto the top rail of the porch, tamped his pipe with a rough finger and pulled at it, getting the tobacco in the bowl to glow scarlet, like next month's leaves. He was nothing if not a patient man. Goodwin would come around to what was troubling him in his own time. Past the corn field and through the trees, sunlight flashed off the waters of a stream where the leaf cover opened enough to disperse the deep forest shadows; shadows that hugged the earth in most every inch of this part of Missouri where a man hadn't yet taken an ax to the land. It was thick timber country, and McKendree loved it as a father loves a child, and respected it as a deadly adversary.

Goodwin said, "I wish young Lucas was turning seventeen or eighteen day after tomorrow, Josh, instead of thirteen."

McKendree looked at him, surprised, and grinned. "You wanting to marry Sarah off already?"

Goodwin laughed. "It's not that at all. It's just that there aren't so many young'uns to choose from in these parts. If Lucas was a bit older, well, he might be able to give someone else competition."

Now Goodwin was getting down to the gristle that was troubling him. "Who you got in mind to give competition to?"

"Jimmy Ribalt."

McKendree lifted an eyebrow. "Jacques Ribalt's oldest boy?"

"He's been hanging around of late. I caught him in the canebrake watching the place last month. I'd seen him behind the barn a few weeks ago, and Sarah told me he stopped her once on the road to talk. I don't know how old that boy is, but he has the grown-up look of a man, and I don't figure he's taken an interest in my place after all these years just to be friendly. His daddy made it clear they don't care for me, nor you, Josh, for that matter. We are all trespassers on their private territory even though we paid hard cash for our land, and got clear title to it."

McKendree whistled softly. "Ribalt's got a streak of mean running clear through him. I'd not be pleased to call him kin."

"And I won't, neither. I've got a mind to ride out to his place and tell him to keep his boy from nosing around my daughter."

"He'll run you off, him and his sons."

Goodwin nodded his head. "He'll try."

McKendree felt the corners of his lips pull down. The Ribalt family had lived in their valley since the time of the French, and Jacques Ribalt didn't recognize any law but his own. McKendree had faced the man a time or two, and always there was one of his sons up a tree with a gun, or his Shawnee wife peeking through the tattered curtains with a rifle ready at hand. Mostly the troubles between them had been over Jacques Ribalt's trap lines. Both McKendree and Goodwin had found spring traps on their property. One of Goodwin's milk cows got hung up in Ribalt's traps only last winter. Their complaints fell on deaf ears. Over the years they'd tried to ignore the man. Confrontation did little good, and stories had it that Jacques Ribalt had taken more than one scalp from men who crossed him.

McKendree said, "I won't tell you what you should or should not do, Charles, but I'd advise you to think clearly on how you intend to handle it."

Goodwin leaned over the railing and let the tension in his frame drain away. More than anything, he needed to talk, and McKendree understood. Life on the western frontier wasn't easy for a man unfettered by obligations; it was harder yet for a man with a family, and a pretty daughter beginning to attract the attentions of the local boys.

"I don't intend to do anything foolish, Josh," he said. Then from within the house came the footsteps of the women. Goodwin glanced back quickly. "Not a word of this to Rachael. I don't want to worry her needlessly."

McKendree nodded his head as Noreen and Rachael stepped out onto the porch. Noreen was a sturdy woman of good Irish stock and McKendree had grown comfortable with her over the last fourteen years. They'd met in St. Louis shortly after he had come to Missouri from Tennessee. They married, bought the farm, and it wasn't long after that that Lucas was born. With the arrival of a son came the reality of commitments and obligations. He threw a harness on his wandering ways and settled down to make a living turning the land. He seldom left the homestead now except to hunt deer and bear for their larder, and turkey for the Thanksgiving and Christmas dinners they always shared with the Goodwins.

Noreen had settled into country life so easily it had amazed him, almost as easily as she fitted into life in the city where her father made a comfortable living silversmithing. She'd given up ease and comfort to move with him to the frontier farm, and he had tried his best never to let her regret it. Now, at thirty, the years had only made her more attractive in his eyes. After bearing him two children, Noreen still had the figure of a twenty-year-old, and carried herself straight and proud. She owned two linsey-woolsey dresses, a linen sunbonnet, two petticoats and a bedgown she had sewn from a fine, soft cotton print Josh had traded for in Jefferson City one year when the hunting had been good. And with that, and Lucas, and him, she was content.

Cupped in her hand against her breast was a little yellow whelp trying to shove a wet nose through her fingers. "What you got there?" McKendree said, leaving the conversation he and Charles Goodwin were having. "One of Lilly's pups?"

Noreen held the squirming ball of fur in the air and glanced at the two dogs romping with the children. She said, "It looks like we know who the pa to these pups is."

Rachael, a shorter, plumper woman with a pretty face, four years older than Noreen, said, "Soon as Lilly had 'em I know'd old Duke had come a courtin'."

"Duke! Duke! Come here, boy!" McKendree said, clapping his hands together with his clay pipe clenched between his teeth. The big yellow dog wheeled about, stopped, cocked an ear then bounded across the yard and up the porch, sliding to a stop and slapping the peeled upright with his tail. The second dog, Duchess, stuck her nose in with her tail fanning the air, and suddenly the porch seemed small for all of them. Noreen sat down on the first step and let the curious animals nuzzle the pup.

"See what you sired, Duke," Noreen said, scratching the big yellow head that made her own hand seem small in comparison. "This here is your son. You gonna take responsibility for him?"

Duke merely looked up at her, his head cocked to one side, and after a sniff at the squirming yellow ball, he and Duchess spun about and bounded headlong after the bouncing iron hoop.

"Guess he ain't gonna claim him," Noreen said, standing.

"Ain't that like a man," Rachael said with half a smile and an arm around Charles' waist.

"Not all men shun their responsibilities," Charles said, feigning resentment, but a smirk gave him away.

Noreen handed the pup to McKendree. "How would you like to have another mouth to feed?" she said, giving him a curious look he wasn't quite sure how to interpret.

He eyed the little ball of fur critically. "It's the runt of the litter."

"Rachael says we can have him once he's weaned."

"Hasn't Lilly got one with a little more meat on its bones?"

"None that look like Duke. The rest are black."

"Hum." McKendree studied the pup a moment longer but he already knew his answer, and so did Noreen. "Well, if you think we need another dog, I suppose this one will do. I'll have to shoot a bear to feed it so as to get some meat on its bones."

"We can name him Little Duke. You can always use another dog when you go hunting."

Josh handed the pup to Rachael, who took it back into the house and put it in the basket among the other sucklings with their wet noses up against Lilly's belly.

The sky was darkening and shadows stretched out beneath the trees. The afternoon was releasing its heat. It was time to be getting home. Noreen gave Rachael a goodbye hug and said she'd see her tomorrow. McKendree told Charles they'd talk later, then he reached inside the cabin for his hunting bag and rifle while Noreen called Lucas to come.

On the road, Lucas skipped ahead with Duke and Duchess. Mc-Kendree levered his long rifle over his shoulder, gripping it by the barrel. He was aware of Noreen's small hand folding into his own. After a minute she spoke.

"Rachael is coming over tomorrow to help me ready the place for Lucas' birthday."

"So I gathered," he said, watching the shadows deepen along the roadside as was his habit. Indians weren't much a problem these days, but there was always room in the larder for extra bear meat or venison. "I'll have to ride into St. Elizabeth tomorrow and pick up that rifle Ben Towers is building for him."

"He'll like that," she said. He heard her uncertainty.

"I was thirteen when I got my first rifle," he said.

"I didn't know that." She fell silent, and after a moment said, "How do you really feel about having another mouth to feed, Josh?"

He grinned down at her and gave her hand a squeeze. "I told you, if you really want that scrawny pup, I don't mind. Beside, dogs aren't extra mouths to feed. Mostly they fend for themselves."

"I'm not talking about a dog, Josh."

McKendree's natural gait carried him on for two more strides before her words drove home and made him pull up short. He looked into her blue eyes that were suddenly wide and shining, like sunlight off pools of water. The twitch at the corner of her lips told him she was having difficulty containing a smile that wanted out.

"What did you say?"

"I said, I wasn't talking about a dog." Suddenly Noreen could control the smile no longer and it burst out and spread across her face. "We're gonna have another baby."

McKendree swept her up in his arms as if she had been no more than eiderdown on a gust of wind and whirled her around and around.

"Josiah McKendree, put me down!" Noreen cried, laughing as the wind took away her bonnet and unfurled her long red hair.

But he ignored her plea and whirled her around until he was too dizzy to continue. Duchess came up the road to investigate, and as they reeled like two drunks on a Saturday night McKendree said, "A baby!" He held her by the shoulders, looking into her face as she tried desperately to comb the hair from her eyes. She managed a nod of her spinning head and was suddenly engulfed in his arms, her face smothered against his linen hunting shirt.

Duke came next and sat down next to Duchess, their tails raising a dust storm upon the road as they watched curiously. Lucas rounded the bend and stopped. Noreen forced herself from her husband's arms and quickly brushed the hair from her eyes, glancing at the road for the wayward sunbonnet.

"What's wrong?" Lucas asked. He had his mother's wide blue eyes, and her faint spattering of freckles across the bridge of his nose. But he had McKendree's dark hair, and the long gangling arms and legs that promised he would grow into the tall, powerful man his father was.

"Your ma and I were just talking."

"Talking about what?"

McKendree glanced at Noreen. She nodded her head. He said, "Your ma is going to have another baby. That means you are going to have a brother, or maybe a sister."

Lucas thought a moment, then said, "Oh," and skipped back down the road with the dogs bounding ahead of him.

Noreen laughed as she tied the bonnet under her chin. Josh picked up his rifle. Their fingers intertwined again as they started once more for home.

"Does Rachael know?"

"Not yet. I wanted to tell you first."

"What took you so long?"

She shrugged her shoulders. "I was just waiting for the right time." She squeezed his hand again, and as the shadows moved across the little two-rut road they were walking, McKendree was suddenly thinking of his youth in Tennessee. He thought of his mother and father, his brothers and sisters, and he wished there had been at least one of them left that he could tell. But they were all gone. That life was gone. All he had now was Noreen and Lucas . . . and the baby of course. He had a home, a hundred and twenty acres of rich bottom land to work, and he had good friends.

McKendree decided he had more than most men, and all at once he was content, and happy.

TWO

JACQUES RIBALT tied bear fat to the trigger plate with the precision of a surgeon about to take a scalpel to a carbuncle. When he had finished, it would have taken a mighty tug to remove the bait, mighty enough to spring the trap and drive the iron jaws together in a death grip no fox or opossum or raccoon could escape. Satisfied with his handiwork, his black beard rustled apart in a grin revealing holes where teeth once resided. Heaving downward, he compressed the side springs and with his thumbs set the trigger-dog. He eased the pressure, the dog clicked in place, setting the trap, and Ribalt covered it over with leaf litter from the forest floor.

This was the last of them. Twenty-four of Hill's traps at a dollar forty each, strung out, baited, set and anchored to the ground so they couldn't be dragged off. He rubbed the bear grease from his hands as he stood. A bear of a man himself, Ribalt weighed over two hundred and fifty pounds and when he walked the top of his beaver hat bobbed along at just a little over six feet seven inches above the forest floor. A bear claw necklace jangled about his neck and rattled across the beadwork of his shirt. He carried a long, .52 caliber Leman rifle and a fringed hunting bag over his right shoulder. Over his left shoulder hung the empty trap sack and a leather pouch half filled with bear fat and chicken livers.

Despite his bulk, Ribalt's passage through the forest made no sound except for the jangling of the bear claw necklace. But he wasn't hunting, nor was he being pursued, and he felt no great urgency to tuck the ornament into his shirt. He was going home, following a trace that his father before him had worn into the ground. The trace took him up over a ridge where out of long habit he paused to scan the tops of the trees in the valley below.

To his left, and half a mile off, a pillar of gray smoke threaded into the hazy blue sky. Ribalt studied it without smiling. The McKendrees were a thorn in his side—had been since they moved into the valley. Ribalt spat on the ground. He had little use for farmers, or the fences they built. He had no patience for their whining complaints when their livestock wandered into one of his traps. It was his land by inheritance. All his! He put no store in the pieces of paper that said otherwise. The state of Missouri had no more right to divvy up the land than did the farmers. One did it with fences, the other with words on paper. Ribalt would have no truck with either.

He turned back on the path, slinging the rifle over his shoulder as he walked. His moccasins padded the soft forest floor, leaving hardly a trace of his passing despite his great size. From the top of his moccasin he slipped a thin blade free of its hidden scabbard and sliced a chaw from a plug of tobacco. He stuffed it into his mouth, pausing only long enough to return the flat blade to its sheath, nicely out of sight, but never far from his thoughts.

As Ribalt came off the ridge into the valley where his home was, he paused to study the clearing. Chickens scratched the ground, unconcerned about the world around them. Yellow Leaf stepped out of the house and tossed a pan of dishwater into the yard. Jimmy, his eldest, was sharpening an ax on the big wheel beneath the towering elm tree. Jacques had built a platform high up in its branches and a man with a rifle could command a view of the only approach to the house. Antoine, Jacques' second son, was stretching a puma skin in a frame of ash saplings. In another moment Louis, his ten-year-old, stepped into view followed by a dog. Everything appeared normal.

The dog was the first to become aware of the big man's return. It sniffed the wind, then drew tail and trotted off toward the lean-to barn and clambered behind the woodpile there. Louis saw his father emerge from the thick timber. The boy came to an abrupt stop as the big man moved past him with the jangle of beads, the smell of dead animals and the odor of campfire smoke on his buckskins. Louis did not dare to look into the great bearded face for fear of catching his father's eye and perhaps bringing his wrath down upon him. Not that Louis had done anything to warrant Ribalt's wrath; experience had taught him that his father's temper could spark to life at the least provocation—or no provocation at all.

Ribalt strode past his youngest son as if he'd been a figure carved from a block of cottonwood. Antoine momentarily stopped his work. Even the birds seemed to stop singing when Ribalt appeared, and only Jimmy was pleased to see his father return. His long legs stopped pumping the sharpening stone and he set the ax aside.

"How it go, Pa?"

Ribalt paused with a foot on the first step of the porch and swung around to face his eldest son. Of all his children, Jimmy was most like him, and that pleased Ribalt. They thought alike—his other sons took after their mother. Jimmy, at seventeen, was already man-size. His shoulders filled out the linen shirt and his arms were thick and corded from swinging an ax. The Ribalts did not turn the ground. Jacques would permit no farming on his land. Except for the vegetables Yellow Leaf raised in a patch behind the house, and the small square of corn planted alongside the garden, all their needs were supplied by the game he trapped or shot. He traded skins for powder and lead, and anything else they could not produce on their land.

Ribalt studied his son. He liked the defiant gleam in the boy's eyes, his boldness toward him—the other boys kept their distance and watched their tongues. They were much like Yellow Leaf—weak. But he'd work that out of them in due time. Ribalt said, "Got them strung out, boy. Down south a couple miles, just below the ridge line."

"That's a good area, Pa. Close to water."

Ribalt grunted. "We'll see. Go round up your rifle and a sack. We need to check another line."

Jimmy sliced a chaw from his plug and wedged it into the corner of his mouth. "Down by the Goodwin place?" he asked casually.

"That's right, boy."

Jimmy grinned and spat a stream of brown juice at the ground. "I'll be ready in a minute, Pa." He turned to the tack house where he slept.

The boy didn't hurry, but Ribalt understood the special interest the Goodwin place held for him. He had hoped Jimmy would have picked another, one closer akin to the family, but that was his decision. The girl could be made to fit in—anyone could be made to change given enough persuasion. He grinned at the thought, turned back to the house and stopped suddenly. Toward the dusty hard-pack at the foot of the steps his eyes came together, fixed on a patch of ground. When he turned back to the house it was with a renewed caution and a thumb hooked over the hammer spur of his rifle. In the shade on the far side of the yard, Antoine returned to his task of stretching the skins while young Louis came out of his statue-like pose and went off to find the dog.

Yellow Leaf, a full-blood Shawnee, had been given to Ribalt by Yellow Leaf's uncle according to the custom of the tribe of Ribalt's mother. She had been sixteen, and three years orphaned, when he had taken her. She had never loved Ribalt, but then love was never required. She accepted her position as his mate . . . as was the custom of her tribe.

She looked up from the black kettle bubbling over the open hearth as he came through the door. Ribalt glanced around the single room. His view lingered on Yellow Leaf a long moment before he set his rifle by the door jamb. She did not speak, but watched him pull back a chair. She ladled stew into a bowl and set it before him. Ribalt tasted it, glanced up narrowly and said, "It needs salt."

She pushed the wooden dish of salt across the table to him. Ribalt said without looking up, "There's tracks out front. Who's been here?"

She rubbed her hands on her apron. "The preacher man, Russell Daub."

Ribalt grunted and took a spoonful of stew. "What'd he want?"

"He asked if we needed anything."

Ribalt narrowed an eye. "Did you tell the meddler we don't have no need for any of his kind of pious help?"

"I told him you were not at home and that he had best leave before you returned."

"Daub knows he ain't welcome here."

"Russell Daub said he'd be a while in St. Elizabeth if we needed anything."

"He ain't got nothing we need."

Yellow Leaf turned back to the bubbling pot. She had wanted to point out to Ribalt that he had made it clear that no one was welcome at their front door, and that maybe Reverend Russell Daub might have something they needed, but she made no mention of it. There was safety in silence. Once Ribalt's wrath was kindled, there was no dousing it until it had run its course.

Jimmy came in with rifle in hand. "I'm ready, Pa."

Ribalt pushed back the bowl, half eaten, and sleeved the leavings from his beard. He snatched up his rifle and stepped out into the afternoon sunlight. The yard was empty now, as both Antoine and Louis had found other chores that removed them from the proximity of their father. He and Jimmy struck a trace that took them through the deep forest, along the river to where his trap line lay, a short distance from Charles Goodwin's home.

Reverend Russell Daub found no one home at the McKendree place. He tied his horse to the top rail of the porch and settled down in the cane rocking chair to await their return. He made it through this area only twice a year and he didn't want to travel on without having visited all the sheep in his flock.

Daub was a tall, narrow man in his early forties who had begun to use spectacles. He removed them from their protective case as he settled down into the rocker and opened a thick King James Bible upon his lap. Unlike some men, Daub felt no disgrace in having to wear the lenses for reading. Indeed, if they made the study of the Word easier, they were a blessing to be worn proudly.

Later, with the shadows lengthening and the afternoon heat pouring off the land, Daub heard their barking as the dogs bounded into the yard. Duke wheeled to a stop and eyed Daub, his tail suddenly still and his ears stiff and alert. Duchess came happily forward wagging her tail. Lucas skipped into view next, shouldering a tree branch as a rifle and making pretend gunfire sounds at pretend Indians.

"Reverend Daub!" Lucas said, surprised and hefting the pretend rifle over his shoulder as he'd seen his father do a thousand times. "What brings you out?"

Daub folded the heavy book and stood. He clasped Lucas' hand. "My, you've grown since I last was through these parts."

"I'll be thirteen day after tomorrow."

"I remember when you were no bigger than that dog over there."

"Shoot, Reverend, I weren't never that small," Lucas said.

Daub laughed. "Your ma and pa around?"

"They're down the road a mite. Should be along in a few minutes."

"I don't get into this area nearly as often as I'd like, so I'm trying to visit everyone, and see if I can be of any help."

"You mean like picking corn or digging potatoes?"

"Well, not exactly, but yes, if that was the need, I'd certainly roll up my sleeves and pitch in."

"Pa says we need to be getting to it soon now as summer is drawing to a close."

Daub glanced at the field beyond the rail fence. Rows of corn covered three acres of land that McKendree had carved from virgin forest. "Looks like Josiah has himself a fine crop this year."

"We had favorable rain, and I helped a lot," Lucas said, expanding his chest.

"I'm sure you did. Why, the way you're growing it won't be no time before you'll be clearing land of your own." Josh and Noreen came up the road. "Here comes your pa now."

Lucas ran and announced the arrival of the preacher at the house. McKendree picked up his pace and with a smile and a stout handshake, welcomed the visitor into his home.

"I'm just making my visits," Daub said, setting his Bible and hat on the table. "It's a big area and I'm only one man." Daub smiled and accepted the glass of well water Noreen set before him. "Thank you. Tell me, how is it going, Josiah? It appears you have fine crop this year."

"We do. I cleared another acre last fall and put it in seed this spring. Plan to clear another before the snows fly. Lucas is getting old enough to be a big help. Charles Goodwin lends a hand when he is able."

Daub nodded his head. "And how are the Goodwins?"

"They had a favorable year."

"I'll be paying them a visit next, and then I reckon I'll head on over to Henley."

"Henley," Noreen said. "That's some distance off."

"My flock is spread wide and thin," he said. "That's why I don't make it through but twice a year."

"Will you be having services before you leave?" Noreen asked.

"I'd like to. I intend to spend the winter in St. Elizabeth and I plan to schedule regular services."

"Just like a real church," Noreen said, clapping her hands together.

McKendree frowned. "You forget, St. Elizabeth is almost a full day's ride there and back."

Noreen's excitement dulled a bit, then brightened. "But we could make the services sometimes."

"We could do that," he said.

"I know it will be difficult," Daub said, "but with my flock so spread out, it's the best I can do."

"Well," said Noreen, "we will certainly make it to as many services as we can, and you must promise to spend the night with us. It's getting dark and I don't want you wandering about at night when we have a bright, cozy house to offer you."

McKendree stood, grinning, for he knew no one could resist Noreen's hospitality if she saw fit to force it on them. "I'll put up your horse, Reverend," he said, "and you might just as well figure on eating a meal with us too. Noreen won't send a guest to bed without a belly full of victuals."

In the coolness of the evening, McKendree took Daub's horse to the barn. Overhead, the hazy sky was darkening and to the west a red glow remained where the sun had sunk below the horizon. Lucas walked with him, his stick-rifle resting in the crook of his arm. Neither man nor boy felt the need to speak. McKendree stretched out a hand and ruffed Lucas' hair, then opened the barn door and put Reverend Daub's horse in one of two empty stalls.

As he unsaddled the animal, Lucas fed a bucket of grain to the horses and tossed a fork of grass hay into each stall. It was dark when they finished. McKendree was busting vest buttons to tell Daub the good news—but he knew Noreen would make mention of it if she wanted it known. She had a strange set of priorities when it came to whom she would tell and whom she would not, and in what order she'd tell them. McKendree would let her handle it the way she saw fit. Noreen was stirring dinner over the hearth when he stepped through the door. He settled across the table from the preacher, forgoing the jug he usually offered guests. He was anxious to hear what news Daub brought with him from the surrounding farms and towns.

Ribalt removed two coons, a coyote and a gray fox from the string of traps, and as the sun set and the land darkened, he rebaited them, then looked around for Jimmy. The boy was supposed to be helping but almost immediately upon their arrival at the trap line, Jimmy had disappeared. Ribalt found him on the ridge that overlooked the Goodwins' place, sitting on a deadfall, staring down at the cabin in the distance.

"What are you doing, boy?"

Jimmy turned, startled. He had not heard his father's silent approach. "Ah—I ain't doing nothing."

"You was supposed to be helping me with the traps."

Jimmy got to his feet. "I guess I just got distracted. Come on, Pa, let's get to them."

Ribalt let go a stream of tobacco juice through a gap in his teeth and grunted. "It's already finished. I done it myself." He nodded his head at the valley where the stream was now only a black trace on the shadowed landscape. "Something down there catch your eye?"

"No," Jimmy replied too quickly.

Ribalt tugged his beard thoughtfully. He would have smiled if he knew how. Instead, he nodded his head and said, "I wouldn't want you to be keeping anythin' from me, boy."

"I . . . I ain't, Pa."

Ribalt hefted the sack over his shoulder and nodded at Jimmy's rifle against a tree. "Collect your things, boy, and let's get moving."

Jimmy grabbed up his rifle and followed his father off the ridge, but not without first throwing a parting glance over his shoulder at the little cabin in the quiet valley below.

THREE

McKENDREE THREADED the leather strap through the cinch ring on Reverend Daub's saddle and pulled it up tight. The old mare sucked in a belly full of air in defiance to the saddle and gave him a challenging look. But McKendree had played this game before. He bit down on the stem of his clay pipe only to discover the fire in the bowl had gone out. Outside, he fished a match from his pocket and paused a moment in the morning sunlight to study the stick in his fingers. Thornberg had called them lucifers. It seemed a right enough name for a device that would conjure up fire on command. McKendree had traded a bear hide and twenty pounds of lard for five pounds of gunpowder, thirty pounds of lead, six shaped flints and one box of these new matches at Thornberg's Mercantile. They seemed more a novelty than anything else, and he still kept his tinder kit dry and handy.

The match flared in his fingers. He put it to the tobacco, drawing deeply. At the house, Noreen moved past the open doorway, busily putting together a sack of corn dodgers for Reverend Daub. Noreen needed the touch of the outside world more than he. It was something he could easily live without. All he required was his family, his home and the occasional visit from friends like Daub or Charles Goodwin. But Noreen had been raised in St. Louis; she missed the bustle of people, the traffic of busy streets, the fancy stores where anything a soul desired could be purchased.

He stepped back inside the barn and eyed the horse. The cinch strap now hung loose about her belly as she munched hay. He smiled around the stem of the pipe. He could have fought her, but a little patience had saved him the effort. He took up the slack in the cinch without objection and led the animal around to the house. Noreen put the sack of corn dodgers in Daub's hand only after he vowed to return soon.

"I'll let you know about the new church," he said as he climbed atop the old mare. He turned the horse toward the road and started away. He drew rein suddenly and seemed to peer at something obscured by the trees. In another moment Charles Goodwin came into view. Goodwin pulled his horse in from a trot and the two men spoke briefly. From the porch, McKendree saw the urgency in his friend's manner.

"What is it?" Noreen said, instinctively dropping a hand on Lucas' shoulder.

"I don't know." McKendree stepped off the porch and strode long-legged across the yard.

"Mornin', Josh," Goodwin said.

"Charles. What brings you out this early?"

Goodwin reached behind his saddle and came back holding a spring trap. "There's a string of these back behind my place. On *my* land!"

McKendree frowned. It wasn't as if this had been the first time Ribalt's traps had been found on their land. Talking to the man didn't help matters. Ribalt hated the farmers, and no amount of talking was ever going to change that. "What are you intending to do about it, Charles?"

Goodwin hefted the rifle he carried across his saddle. "I'm gonna talk to that man in the only language he understands." Goodwin's eyes narrowed. "We've both had problems with him stringing traps on our land, Josh." He paused. "I was sort of hoping you'd ride along with me."

"Now wait a minute, Charles," Daub broke in, "can't we find a different way to go about this? Perhaps if you'd let me talk to—"

"Ribalt don't listen to talk, Reverend," he said.

McKendree said, "There is more to this than just some of Ribalt's traps on your land, isn't there, Charles?"

Goodwin reared back in his saddle and his back stiffened. "You know the problems I'm facing, Josh."

McKendree sucked on the pipe and blew a puff of smoke in the still morning air. "I'll ride with you, but maybe it would be a good idea if Daub comes along. He's good at talking. I'd rather we handle this with talk than with that smoke pole."

Goodwin looked at Daub. "No offense, Reverend, but this is a personal matter."

Daub returned Goodwin's glance with an intense stare of his own. "The problems of my flock are my problems, Charles. I'd like to help."

Goodwin thought this over. McKendree said, "I think the Reverend ought to know, Charles."

Slowly he nodded his head. "Maybe you're right. All right, you're welcome to come, and if you can help, it will be appreciated."

Daub smiled. "That's what I'm here for, Charles."

"I'll get my horse," McKendree said and walked back to the house to tell Noreen what had come up. He saddled his horse in the corral. "I'll have to run into St. Elizabeth tomorrow for Lucas' birthday present, Noreen," he said when she came to him at the barn.

"It's not important. What's important is that you be careful."

He gave her a reassuring grin. "We're just going out to talk to the man."

"You know how he is, Josh—crazy and wild. No telling what he might do."

"Reverend Daub will be along. I don't expect trouble."

Noreen stood on her toes and kissed him. "Just the same, you be careful."

He stuck his moccasin into the stirrup and swung up. "I will. You take care here. I'll be back in a couple hours."

Noreen watched the three men ride off. An uneasiness weighed her spirit. He'd gone off many times, and always she worried until the easy gait of his horse carried him home again . . . but this time the feeling was heavier. Unexplainably, it made her want to shout and call him back—but she didn't. She stood in the growing morning heat long after he'd disappeared from her view, feeling the humidity build in the air, unaware of the swarms of black gnats that were as much a part of late summer as the heat and the afternoon thunderstorms. With a shrug of her shoulders, she moved the concern aside, gathered up her skirts and, feeling the cool, dusty earth beneath her toes, returned to her house and the chores of the day.

McKendree took the lead when the trace through the woods narrowed. Single file beneath the cover of leaves where sunlight managed to touch the ground in scattered bright patches, Goodwin filled Reverend Daub in on the recent appearances of Jimmy Ribalt around their farm, and the worries it had kindled within him. Daub listened without comment, except to spur Goodwin on when he lapsed into drawn-out silence. McKendree listened to the conversation with only part of his attention, the greater portion of it riveted on the shifting shadows within the forest, and the sounds of the birds and squirrels.

For the moment the sounds were normal, and the shadows not threatening. He'd been to Ribalt's place only a few times, and always the trapper seemed to know of his arrival beforehand. McKendree never discovered how the man managed to learn of his comings, but he was determined he'd not be forewarned today. He drew up. Behind him Goodwin and Daub brought their horses to a halt. "What is it, Josiah?" Daub asked.

"We are almost there," he said, peering through the trees. "I don't want to announce our coming if I can help it."

Daub nodded. Goodwin drew in a breath and said, "Let's get on with it."

There was reluctance in Goodwin's tone, and McKendree wondered if he'd have come at all if he had to do it alone. Ribalt's reputation was well known, and most men preferred to avoid the trapper. He urged his horse forward. Their talking ceased. The only sound of their passage was the muffled footfall of their horses' hooves upon the blanket of humus beneath them.

The trees opened up. In the distance a clearing came into view. McKendree stopped at the edge of it and surveyed the cluttered yard. Frames of hides drying in the shade stood off to one side near where the trees began again. A lean-to barn sat at the back of the yard near a tack shed and a smokehouse. The log cabin had an added-on look to it, and scraps of iron and coils of chains were piled alongside it. An old sharpening wheel huddled beneath the boughs of an elm tree; a chopping block with an ax wedged into it occupied the middle of the yard. There was a pile of new-split wood beside it. The yard was deserted, but the skin behind McKendree's right ear began to itch. No wind blew to stir the dust about the house. The gray smoke from the chimney rose straight into the air. Chickens scratched and clucked and pecked at the ground. The curtain in the window moved briefly as if touched by the wind, only . . .

McKendree tightened his grip about the neck of his rifle as he urged his horse into the yard and stopped in front of the cabin. Goodwin moved up on his left, Daub took the other side.

"It's your show, Charles," he said. The curtain had stopped moving and there was an unnatural silence about the place. The front door of the cabin remained closed. McKendree knew unseen eyes watched them.

Goodwin hesitated, then leaned forward in his saddle and called, "Ribalt! I want to talk with you."

They waited. Heat rose from the open ground, heavy with the scent of dust and wood chips. A fly buzzed in the still air. Goodwin glanced at McKendree, then back to the closed door.

"Ribalt!"

The wooden latch lifted and the door swung inward. For a moment the open doorway remained a shadowed rectangle, then Jacques Ribalt filled it, stepping heavily outside. His black beard glistened in the sunlight, his dark eyes all but hidden beneath the brim of his hat. He carried his rifle in both hands, cocked and ready. The necklace of bear claws about his neck glistened in the morning light like polished ivory fish hooks.

McKendree pulled himself up in his saddle to almost the same degree that Goodwin shrank back into his own. Ribalt might intimidate some men, but McKendree knew it was a mistake to show it.

Ribalt's eyes lingered a moment on the preacher, then found a place to rest in McKendree. The two men assessed each other until Ribalt broke it off and directed his attention to Goodwin. "What brings you into my valley?" he said in a voice that might have arisen from the bottom of a barrel.

Goodwin dropped the trap to the ground. "I found this, and more of 'em, on my property, Ribalt. I don't mind you working the area, but keep 'em off my land."

Ribalt eyed the trap lying in the dust. He shifted his view back to

Goodwin. "I set my traps where I please, and I don't like them fooled with." His fingers tightened around the rifle.

McKendree eased his own rifle off the saddle and inched the muzzle around.

"You three get off my land or I'll bury you here."

Daub said, "Wait a minute, Mr. Ribalt. Charles has a valid complaint and I think it would be to everyone's interest if we could talk about it and come to some mutually agreeable resolution of the problem."

Ribalt's rifle came around and centered on Daub. "I don't need no interference from the likes of you, preacher man. When I want anything from you I will come and get you. Meantime, you and your friends get off my land."

"Put the rifle up, Ribalt." McKendree's voice was low, and flint hard.

The Frenchman swiveled his eyes at the rifle pointing at him. His lips peeled back into a slow smile and the rifle in his hand came around in a standoff.

McKendree watched his eyes, ready to move in an instant, but Ribalt just stood there, laughing low through his beard. "Jimmy, Antoine," he called.

McKendree caught the movement out of the corner of his eye. Goodwin swiveled in his saddle. When he settled back around he said, "Best put up the gun, Josh. Ribalt has his boys up a tree behind us."

McKendree's view remained fixed upon Ribalt. "Tell them to put up their guns."

"The devil I will, McKendree," Ribalt rumbled, his black eyes unblinking.

"Josiah," Daub said, "This is no way to handle it."

"Listen to your preacher friend, McKendree. Listen to him or die."

"Josiah!" Daub said with swelling urgency.

The curtain in the window parted and another rifle poked out. Behind it, Yellow Leaf sighted down the barrel.

McKendree could take Ribalt with his first shot, but none of them would ride out alive. The price to satisfy his building anger was too high. Restraining the bile that climbed to his throat, he eased the hammer down to the pan and raised his weapon.

Ribalt laughed. "Now get out of here before I have my boys blow you all to hell."

"Let's go, Josh," Goodwin said in a low, bitter voice.

McKendree leaned forward. "You keep your traps off of our land or I'll be back."

McKendree reined his animal around, and glancing up the tree to the platform where the two boys knelt with their rifles to their shoulders, he rode away. Goodwin and Daub kept at his heels as the trees closed behind them, and for a good distance they heard Ribalt's rumbling laughter ring through the forest like a taunting ghost chasing them away.

FOUR

THE AX struck a glancing blow off the gnarled tree trunk, shaving off mere slivers. Wide wedges would have flown if the tree had been of any other ancestry than oak. The ancient wood resembled solid rock. McKendree's muscles bunched beneath the linen hunting shirt and the ax whistled through the air. The thud ricocheted off the back side of the cabin and out into the forest. He swung back and took aim. The blade flashed through the air, and again only thin slivers shaved away beneath its driving blow. From the corner of the house Noreen watched him pull back and swing out. Sweat beaded on his forehead and soaked his shirt.

"Josh," she said finally, coming to him.

The ax paused, mid-stride.

"It's too hot for this now."

He turned back to the stubborn tree and completed his swing. The air reverberated with the blow. "That man can be so infuriating, Noreen," he said, taking aim again.

"I know, Josh. There is no talking to the likes of Jacques Ribalt. You can't blame yourself for it going badly this morning."

"I let him get the drop on me. I rode right into it. I shouldn't have allowed that." The ax swung and its blade drove a quarter inch into the tree trunk.

Noreen put a hand on his shoulder. "Put the ax up, Josh. Come back to the house."

McKendree looked into her calm face and felt the anger inside him drain away. Her gentle touch, as always, seemed to soothe the untamed animal that lurked beneath the loving husband and father.

That other man, that animal, wanted to dive for Ribalt's throat with teeth and fangs bared. . . . He let go of the anger and swung the ax one last time and left it where it wedged in an angle of the tree.

Noreen took his hand and gave it a squeeze. "Someday you will chop that tree down," she said.

"I hope not—leastwise, not anytime soon."

"Why not?"

"I'll have to find something else to take an ax to."

"Plenty of trees about, Josh."

He grinned at her. "But none quite so defiant, none that fight back like that old son of Noah."

He and Noreen walked around to the front of the house, where Reverend Daub and Charles Goodwin were sitting on the porch. Rachael stood in the doorway listening to the men talk, keeping one eye on the children playing hide-and-seek near the barn.

McKendree pulled around a chair and Noreen and Rachael went inside the house. "Feel better, Josh?" Goodwin asked.

He filled his pipe and struck a lucifer on the edge of his chair. "I'd feel a whole lot better if I had gotten my fingers around that man's neck."

"Now, Josiah," Daub said, "the Scriptures tell us we are to love our fellow man, no matter how bone-headed and irascible he might be."

He grinned and blew out a cloud of smoke. "The words sound good, Reverend, but in real life they are mighty hard to live by."

"If they were easy words, how much would a man grow in following them. It's only in the trials of life, Josiah, does a man grow."

McKendree grunted and sucked on his pipe. "Plenty of trials out here without adding Jacques Ribalt on top of them."

Daub smiled serenely and lightly drummed his fingers on the thick black book upon his lap. He knew when he was fighting a losing battle. "Sorry I wasn't more help back there. I thought maybe I could reason with Ribalt."

"You can't reason with a stone," Goodwin said.

From behind the barn Lucas ran into view and wheeled to a stop by the porch. "Pa, have you seen Duchess and Duke? We want them to play chase-the-wheel with us."

McKendree leaned forward in the cane chair and scanned the

field of tawny corn, and beyond it to the trees that rose in a solid brown and green wall at the far end. "Last I saw of them they had treed a coon."

"I ain't seen them all day, Pa."

It occurred to McKendree that neither had he. Their coon treeing episode had happened early that morning, before he and Daub and Goodwin had ridden off to see Ribalt. "I reckon they went off hunting somewhere, son. They'll most likely show up before too long."

Lucas cupped his hands and yelled, "Duke! Duchess!" and getting no response he went off to tell the others that the dogs wouldn't be playing this time.

Daub glanced at the angle of the sun. "Well, if I don't get moving I won't make Henley until after dark." He stood and stuck his head into the house to say goodbye to Noreen and Rachael. Noreen made him promise he would send word when church services were to begin, and she checked that he had his sack of corn dodgers before he climbed aboard his mare. With hugs, handshakes and waves, he departed in the heat of the afternoon.

They watched the spot on the road where the trees had swallowed him up, then Rachael stepped next to Charles and said, "Noreen has exciting news."

"Oh?" He pulled his eyes from the bend in the road. "What sort of news?"

"She's expecting again."

His look of mild interest turned to a sudden, wide smile. "Why, that's wonderful, Noreen," he said. He gave her a hug, and shook McKendree's hand, and offered his congratulations all around.

"What are you hoping for, a boy or girl?"

"We don't much care, so long as it's healthy," McKendree said, putting an arm around Noreen's waist and drawing her near. "Though another girl would be nice." He saw Noreen's blue eyes turn suddenly sad. She was remembering Mary too, not that the baby they had lost in its infancy was ever far from her thoughts. They had had her only three months before that morning when Noreen discovered her in her crib. Mary had not shown any sign of being ill—and McKendree didn't believe she ever really was sick.

Just one of those things, he told himself after it had happened; an act of God and only God knew the reasons why.

Later that evening, when the Goodwins had left for home and the sun was drifting to the west, McKendree and Lucas walked out to the rear of the corn field. They stopped every so often to call for the dogs, then walk over to another corner and call again. Last year's leaves crunched beneath their moccasins and it wouldn't be but another couple weeks before a new layer would begin to fall to cover up the old one. McKendree looked at the tall corn as they traversed the field, weighing in his mind the chore of harvesting it, of turning the stalks back into the ground.

He stopped at one point, called for Duke and Duchess, then waved a hand at a section of timber and said, "Luke, next month we'll get started clearing this piece of land. That will give us another acre to put into crops." He glanced at the ridge that rose a short distance north of the corn and studied the neat rows of potatoes planted there. They'd have food enough for winter this year. He remembered the hard years he and Noreen had struggled through when they first cleared the land for the cabin and dug a small patch for vegetables.

That seemed such a long time ago. Now the land was producing and their root cellar was full. He still had to hunt for the meat, for lard and for the pelts that kept them warm in the winter and provided trade goods in town, but hunting was a pleasure—his private step back to when he was younger, and on his own . . . when Indians moved about the countryside in painted war parties, and a long knife and dry powder meant the difference between life and death. Hunting allowed him to feel that exhilaration while all the time retaining the comfort and security of a family and a home.

It was dusk when they climbed the single step to the porch. The dogs had still not returned home and that was not their way. Noreen stood by the door wiping her hands on her apron.

"Where do you suppose those two got off to, Josh?"

"No telling," he said, shutting and bolting the door against the darkness outside. It was unusual, but then they were both strapping dogs and he figured they'd come trotting back, footsore from their wanderings, in the morning.

FIVE

THE IMPATIENT SCRATCHING at the door awakened McKendree. He sat up in bed and glanced at the dark window. Noreen turned beneath the covers.

"What is it, Josh?" she asked, half asleep.

"Sounds like the dogs are back and wanting in."

"In?" Noreen came full awake. "They never want in at night. What time is it?"

McKendree threw off the cover and leaned near the back window. "Early. Maybe four." He went to the front window where the porch was still a black rectangle beneath the stars. The moon had gone down, and to the east a faint light had begun to mellow the night sky. He lifted the latch and opened the door. Duchess pushed in, alone, and sat in the middle of the dirt floor thumping her tail.

"You're home mighty late, young lady," he said, scratching her behind the ear.

She stood, turned a circle and bolted out the door.

"Where is Duke?" Noreen asked, wrapping a robe about her.

McKendree stepped out into the night and called the dogs. Duchess came back inside and sat down impatiently, her tail beating double time. "Where is Duke, girl?"

She put her paws on his chest and her ears swiveled forward. McKendree pushed the animal down and knelt beside her in the dark. He touched a spot that was darker than the rest of the yellow fur. "Noreen, bring a candle."

He held the light close to the dog. Duchess started for the door again. McKendree made her sit. "Hold on a minute, girl, what have you gotten into?"

"It looks like blood, Josh."

"It is blood." McKendree peered out the door. "Where is Duke, girl?"

The dog bolted, stopped in the yard and wheeled back as if waiting to be followed.

"I better go see what has happened." He dressed, grabbed up his rifle and hunting bag and set the felt hat upon his head. In ten minutes he and Duchess were into the woods, moving through the darkness. Soon the ground rose beneath his feet. He was climbing the ridge at the far end of his property. Duchess ran ahead, stopped and waited for him to catch up. The sky grew brighter.

Atop the ridge he struck upon a path and picked up his pace. After a while Duchess veered off it and started down the other side. She stopped and began to bark. McKendree angled toward the sound and found her standing over a still shape lying on the ground.

He set his rifle aside and went to his knees. The matted fur beneath his fingers was cold and stiff, and he knew what he was feeling was dried blood. The growing morning light was enough that he could see the dull nothingness in the dog's wide eyes, the drawn stiffness in his pulled-back lips. The teeth were clenched in a death grip, and between them the black iron links of a chain. Duke's leg was a twisted wreckage of blood and tissue. At the point where it was locked in the jaws of an iron spring trap, the desperate animal had attempted to gnaw the limb free. Death had claimed him first.

McKendree eased the lifeless head back to the ground. Within him an animal rage began welling up from the prison he normally kept securely locked. An uncontrollable anger burst forth even as the new light of morning was touching the tree tops and setting the leaves afire with yellow-green brilliance. He ripped the trap from its anchor and one after the other, sprung the entire line. Slinging the two dozen traps over his shoulder, he carried them to the wide stream that flowed nearby and flung them far out into the sluggish water.

Afterward, his anger abated only marginally, McKendree retraced his steps and gathered the dead dog into his arms. Duchess remained at his side, no longer romping, no longer in a hurry, somehow knowing that Duke would not run and play with her.

Whether she understood that it was Ribalt who was responsible, McKendree couldn't know. The important thing was that he knew. . . .

McKendree buried Duke behind the house, not far from the other grave, then he disappeared inside the house. He emerged with his rifle. The long-knife that had been a traveling companion for years hung at his side.

"Where are you going?" Noreen asked, even though the answer to her question was plainly engraved in the deep lines that creased McKendree's face, making him look years older than the man who had awakened beside her that morning.

"Josh, don't."

He started across the yard to the barn. Lucas stood by his mother's side, knowing something foreign had invaded his father. Noreen caught the sleeve of his shirt.

"Josh!"

He wheeled about. Noreen's blue eyes hardened to crystalline ice, faint lines radiating from their corners. For a moment McKendree's heart seemed to stop beating. Only a time or two in the past had he seen such intensity in his wife, and it took that fire within her now to drive back the animal that had taken control of him. . . . His heart marched back into step with the rhythm of his life, only the cadence had changed—the beat was no longer a drumroll call to battle. Her touch, as always, had driven the beast back to its lair deep within his soul.

"What will it accomplish, Josh?"

"He's been told, Noreen," he said, wanting desperately to summon up his beast again, but suddenly unable to. She wouldn't allow that. She never did.

"And what good will telling him again do?" She dropped her eyes to the rifle in his hand. "Unless you intend to do more than talk."

He looked at the rifle and suddenly knew that he had never really intended to use it at all. And Noreen was correct. Talk did no good where Ribalt was concerned.

"Going to him now, like this, will get you killed, Josh. You're too decent a man to shoot Ribalt over a dog, no matter how much you loved that animal. But can you say the same for him? He'd shoot you as soon as look at you, and he'd dance on your grave afterward."

McKendree marveled at her grasp of the truth. She had always been able to see beyond the moment whereas he had used up most of his youth acting on impulse—until she became part of his life. And for the most part life had become easier to live since. But there was still the anger that had to be dealt with, and he knew of only one way to do that.

It took most of an hour, and the old oak tree behind the house had lost a good ten inches of its iron-like wood before he swung the ax one last time and left its blade buried in its heart. McKendree sleeved the sweat from his brow and went to the well for a ladle of water. Lucas had fashioned a cross for Duke's grave and carved his name with a pocketknife. McKendree hunkered down beside the boy and studied his handiwork.

"That looks like a fine memorial to old Duke," he said.

"What's a memorial, Pa?"

"A memorial is something that helps you remember a person . . . or a dog."

"I won't need a memorial to help me remember old Duke."

He gave the boy a smile. "I don't guess I'll need one neither, son, but they're nice to have anyway. Come on, let's get your ma and put it up."

"Pa?"

"Yes?"

"Why didn't you go after Ribalt like you wanted to?"

"Because your ma talked sense into me."

"You weren't scared, were you?"

He looked at Lucas' wide blue eyes, Noreen's eyes, and at the strong, square jaw and chin that could not be mistaken as coming from him, and said, "No, I wasn't scared, and that was the real problem because I should have been."

Lucas wasn't certain he had understood entirely what his father was telling him, but he did feel there was a deeper meaning to his words that a few more years would make clear to him.

They set up the cross and Noreen said a few words over the grave. Lucas remained awhile, looking at the mound of fresh dirt. A short distance away was another grave, overgrown by grass. The carefully fashioned wooden cross that stood watch over it had turned gray over the years and was beginning to crack and warp from the sun and rain and snow. At the head of Mary's grave was the young oak tree McKendree had planted as a memorial, even though, as Lucas had said, no memorial was needed to remember.

Noreen took Josh aside. "I wish this didn't have to happen at all —especially the day before his birthday. We've had so many hard years; I was hoping this one we could give him a birthday that was special."

"All birthdays are special to a little boy if they are celebrated in love. It's only us adults that worry about making them important with gifts." They started slowly toward the house.

She looked up at him with mild amusement and said, "Since when did you become a philosopher?"

He grinned and put an arm around her waist. "Since marrying you. I couldn't stay a bumbling frontiersman very long with such sophistication suddenly come in upon my life."

They laughed and the sadness of the morning seemed to dissipate like the lifting of a ground fog. McKendree said, "Besides, there is that rifle Ben Towers is building for Luke. I figure it will be a right fine birthday present and will take the boy's mind off today's trials."

Noreen frowned despite herself. "I'm not sure a thirteen-year-old is ready for a real gun, Josh. I know, we talked it over and you seem convinced he's old enough and responsible enough, but it still seems young to me."

"You look at Luke as your little baby. He's growing up right before your eyes and you don't see it."

Her frown lengthened. "No, Josh, I do see it. That's part of the problem. I see it and I want to stop it."

"And the gun is one more step up the ladder to manhood?"

She nodded her head and stopped at the front door of their house, turning to face him. "I don't want to lose him too soon. He's all we have."

"We aren't going lose him, Noreen, and he isn't all we have. There is a new life growing inside you. There will be another little one who will depend on you, and a whole new set of birthdays to celebrate."

She smiled faintly and then the smile faded. "I know," she said, "but I can't help thinking about Mary."

McKendree gave her a hug. "We won't lose this one."

She laid her head on his chest and prayed silently that he was right.

SIX

JOSIAH McKENDREE awoke before daylight and dove into his chores to make room in the day for the long ride into St. Elizabeth that morning. It was Lucas' birthday today, and he knew how important that was to both Noreen and his son. When he was growing up, his family merely noted a birthday's passing and then went about the more immediate job of staying alive in a land torn apart first by the war to sever England's yoke, and then later by battles against the Indians led by Tecumseh and Tenskwatawa.

But Noreen's family had made an event of birthdays, and every year it gnawed at her—even though she worked hard at keeping it to herself—that they could not afford to do more for Lucas than a fancy cake and new britches or shoes. This year was going to be different. There was extra money in the tin above the door lintel, and a surplus crop in the field.

Noreen had wheat cakes and coffee ready when he returned from the spring house where he put up the milk. She turned from the stove, her one concession to civilized life, and a gift from her father, when McKendree came in and sat at the table. "I'll be leaving shortly," he said. "Lucas still asleep?"

Noreen glanced up at the loft, where a tick mattress showed through the wide-spaced floor boards. "He had a long and trying day yesterday."

McKendree spread lard on a wheat cake. "We all had a trying day." He didn't want to think of Ribalt today.

"I want today to be special for him," she said, sitting across the table, watching him taste his coffee and reach for a second cake. "When do you expect to be back, Josh?"

"Sometime late this afternoon. I've a few things to tend to while in town, but I'll be prompt and be back before you all get to celebrating."

"Rachael is coming with the kids at noon. Charles will be by later. Do try to hurry, Josh."

He grinned and reached for her hand. "I'll work that old plug into a lather if that's what you want."

She smiled and returned to her stove. "You don't have to punish the horse. Just promise me you'll be careful."

"I promise. I'll be careful."

The sun had but touched the tree tops with its morning light when McKendree saddled up their one horse and gave Noreen a kiss goodbye. Lucas came out the door, sleepy-eyed, and waved goodbye to his father as he rode away. At his heels, Duchess trotted along. McKendree reined in a few rods from the house and told the dog to stay, but she refused, so he shrugged and let her come.

Some miles away Jacques Ribalt was leaving his house too, an empty sack over his shoulder for the animals he hoped to find in the traps, a bag of bait at his waist to reset the line. He paused on his journey atop the ridge to squint at the chimney smoke rising into the air from a place in the forest where as a boy he and his father had set their traps without the interference of neighbors. His lips curled as he turned away and resumed his journey to the trap line he had set out a few days before.

He angled off the ridge toward the river and temporarily forgot about the McKendrees and Goodwins as he searched for blaze on the tree trunk that marked the start of the line. He found his mark in short order and looked about for the first trap. In a few moments he knew the trap had been carried away. He'd have to spend time searching for it later, and he cursed himself for not staking it down more securely. With a snort that sent the black beard ruffling about his lips, he paced off a dozen steps to where the second trap had been set.

He turned the litter of the forest floor with a stick, and in a moment his eyes narrowed to a suspicious scowl. One trap dragged off by a wounded animal was acceptable, but two. . . . His thoughts went back to the visitors and their demands that he keep his traps—his livelihood—off their property. With a surge of apprehension, Ribalt strode down the hill toward the third trap. It was gone too. Like a humped-back bear, he followed the length of the trap line. They were all gone! He retraced his steps and found the place where an animal had bled, and a man had knelt.

Instantly it became clear to him, and his thoughts clouded over with a blood-red rage. With the swiftness of a cat, he bounded up the hill and over its top, consumed with a blind fury that drove him on toward the little cabin in the woods.

"Lucas," Noreen called, standing by the heavy table with a hay broom in her hand. "Lucas, come in here. I can use a hand."

The boy poked his head in the doorway. "What, Ma?"

"Help me move this table so I can sweep under it."

Lucas grabbed one end and they pushed it to one side. "Anything else, Ma?"

"Stay close, I'll need to move it back in a minute."

Lucas sat in a chair by the stove and said, "I wish Duchess had stayed home. I ain't got no one to play with."

Noreen looked up at her son as she swept the dirt floor. "Sarah and Tommy will be along shortly to play. You can spend the next few hours helping me get this place ready for *your* birthday."

"Yes, ma'am," he said with a decided lack of enthusiasm. "When will Pa be home?"

"Sometime this afternoon."

"Why did he have to go to St. Elizabeth today, anyway?"

Noreen held back a grin. Even though she didn't entirely approve of it, she knew the rifle would make this Lucas' best birthday ever. Josh had promised he'd train Lucas in the proper handling and respect for the weapon. Her fears were only a motherly concern, she told herself for perhaps the hundredth time. She said, "Your Pa had some important business to tend to, but he promised to be back this afternoon so he won't miss the party. Now, help me move this table back in place."

Lucas hopped off the chair but stopped in his tracks when a voice boomed outside the door.

"McKendree! Josiah McKendree, show yourself, you cowardly son of a dog!"

Lucas looked at his mother and saw her wide eyes riveted upon the door.

"McKendree!"

Noreen stepped to the window. "It's Ribalt," she said, reaching over and lowering the inside bar across the door.

"What's he doing here?"

"I don't know. . . ."

The heavy door rattled on its hinges.

Noreen took Lucas by his shoulders and held him close. "What is it you want?" she said.

"I want McKendree!" Ribalt said.

"He ain't here—"

"You're lying!" Ribalt drove his shoulder into the door. Noreen backed toward the stove, as if the sound of his shoulder, like a battering ram, had physically driven her back.

"I told you, Josh ain't here." Her eyes expanded as the door bulged inward.

"I ain't leaving without him!"

Then the battering stopped. Noreen felt her heart thumping within her. Lucas said, "Maybe he's gone away," barely above a whisper.

"I wouldn't count on it," she said, whispering too. All at once window glass crashed in upon the floor and the cane chair sailed into the cabin. Right behind it was Ribalt hunkering through the window. Noreen's fingers dug into Lucas' shoulders.

Ribalt straightened up with his rifle swinging from side to side. "Where are you, McKendree?" he demanded. "Where are my traps?"

Noreen turned to stone, her muscles refusing to budge as the rifle came around to rest on her and Lucas. She fought down her terror and said, "Get out of my house, Ribalt."

Two steps brought him across the floor. He smelled of bear fat and smoke, and hovered over her like a black storm cloud. When he grabbed her arm and shook, she thought her teeth would shatter.

"Where are my traps?"

"I don't know what you are talking about," she said, mustering courage that wasn't really there.

His back-handed slap wrenched her head around.

"You leave my mother alone!" Lucas cried and kicked out, catching Ribalt on the shin in a glancing blow.

He lifted the boy off the floor by the front of his shirt and tossed him across the room. Turning back, he hit Noreen again. "Your man took my traps. I want 'em back."

Noreen struggled to speak, to tell him she knew nothing of the matter, but the back of his hand stung her cheek and staggered her back against the hot stove.

Lucas hurled himself at Ribalt. The trapper absorbed the blow with hardly a glance and kicked him back across the room. Noreen reached for a pot of water on the stove. He slapped it from her hand and buried his fist in her stomach. She buckled and went to her knees. Lucas grabbed for his father's tomahawk from the shelf and Ribalt swung his rifle around and fired.

Noreen screamed with shock and terror, and threw herself at Ribalt, her fingers clutching at the bear claw necklace that hung upon his chest. The butt of his rifle came around, driving into her temple, and she dropped to the floor.

He stood there a moment consumed by his rage. There was a smear of blood upon the floor by Noreen's head. His finger reached out and touched blood on the rifle and all at once his thinking cleared. He turned, cat-like, toward the door to listen. Assured that no one had heard the struggle and the gunshot, he searched the cabin. When he found no traps he made his way out the door and back into the safety of the forest.

SEVEN

YELLOW LEAF was surprised to see her husband home so soon. She had expected him to be away much longer. When he worked his traps he sometimes stayed away all day. Immediately, she saw that something was not right with him. He stormed into the cabin and started throwing supplies into a sack.

"Jacques, you are going away?" she asked when he showed no sign that he had seen her standing there.

"Where is Jimmy?" he said, packing powder and shot.

"Out."

He glared at her with a fierceness that set Yellow Leaf back a step. "Find him."

She went to the door and called to Antoine. "Go find Jimmy. Tell him to come here." She looked back at Ribalt with her arms folded resolutely in front of her. "Tell me, Jacques, what has happened?"

Ribalt packed a pouch of tobacco on top of his kit, pushed the sack aside, fell heavily into a chair at the table and began to draw a fine edge on his butcher knife with a whetstone. Yellow Leaf's black eyes fixed upon him until he finally looked up at her.

"I ask you again, Jacques. What has happened?"

"Nothing. I am going away for a spell."

"This is not the season that you go away," she said.

"Well, I am going anyway, woman! Do not question me."

"I will know the answer," she said boldly, knowing her words could bring instant retribution from the man sitting at her table.

Ribalt picked up the pace of his sharpening as if punishing the whetstone beneath the blade for his own sins. He said, "I had trouble. I will have to be gone for a little while. There will be someone coming that I will have to deal with. Afterward, I will return."

"What kind of trouble?"

He did not answer her.

"You killed someone?" she said, seeming to know the truth by his silence.

He looked up from sharpening the knife. "I am not sure. Yes, I think so. Even if I did not, he will come. I must lead him away from here, to some place I can deal with him."

Yellow Leaf's eyes narrowed. "Who is this man that will be coming?"

Ribalt resumed his sharpening. "McKendree."

Her breathing caught. She sat across the table from him. "And who is it you might have killed?"

"His boy. Maybe his woman." He shoved the butcher knife back into its sheath and went to work on the thin, finely balanced blade he carried hidden in the top of his knee-high moccasin.

"You want to see me, Pa?" Jimmy said, stepping into the cabin.

Ribalt kept his eyes on the sliver of steel sliding across the stone. He said, "Get your things together. We are going to be gone for a spell."

Yellow Leaf started to protest. Ribalt cut her off with a glance.

"Where we going?"

"I'm not sure yet. Maybe up to the Shawnee town where your grandpa lives."

"Why?"

Ribalt shot the boy a narrow glance. Jimmy backed out the door without pressing the question. "I'll get my things, Pa."

"Why are you taking Jimmy?" Yellow Leaf asked when the boy had gone.

"Another pair of eyes."

"And you will teach him to kill, too?"

Ribalt shoved the blade back into its hidden sheath and stood. He heaved the sack across his shoulder. "He'll either learn it from me, or end up dead for not knowing how. If I let you have your way about it, you'd raise my sons to be women." He went outside, where Antoine and Louis watched him from the shade of the elm tree. He called them over.

"I'm going away for a while," he said. "I'm taking your brother with me. We are going to have a visitor shortly and he means us no good. You saw him the other day. The tall man who rode with the preacher. His name is McKendree and he will be wanting to hurt your ma." He nodded his head at the platform built high up the tree. "I want one of you up there at all times. When you see Mc-Kendree, shoot him . . . if you can. If you manage it, come look for me. I'll leave a trace a fool can follow." He turned to Yellow Leaf and said, "Don't you go coddling them. Don't try to stop them from what they have to do."

Jimmy came from the tack shed where he kept his kit. "I'm ready to go, Pa."

Ribalt grunted and gave Yellow Leaf a warning glance; a pointed reminder that she was to follow his instructions. Then he marched off into the woods with Jimmy at his side.

McKendree judged the time to be about four o'clock. He'd be getting home right on time for the celebration. When he was less than a mile from their cabin he picked up his pace and Duchess trotted ahead, keeping just within sight. He looked at the new rifle across his lap, next to his own well-worn weapon. It shone like a new penny in the sunlight, as if with an inner life of its own. The walnut had been carefully polished, and the iron barrel, and the latest development in firearms, the percussion lock, had been browned to such a rich finish that it seemed to McKendree the rifle was built to be looked at instead of used. He grinned and tried to imagine what the piece would look like when Lucas' next birthday rolled around. In a year's time the boy would certainly have worn the newness away. And that was as it should be. A rifle was a tool and ought to be used as such.

He rode into the yard, where the Goodwins' wagon and horse stood out in front of the house. Sarah and Tommy were sitting on the ground by the wheel and didn't look up at him when he reined in. Duchess sniffed around the children, then ran to the front door and scratched.

McKendree grinned down at the kids and said, "You two are looking mighty sober. Did you get in trouble?"

Sarah stared up at him with eyes that looked like she had been crying recently. She shook her head.

McKendree swung off his saddle and hunkered down. "Say, what's wrong with you two? You see old Nick lurking in the wood lot?" He glanced around. "Where is Lucas? Don't tell me he's in hot water too."

Sarah turned her eyes back to the ground and said quietly, "He is in the house, Mr. McKendree."

McKendree stood and his grin disappeared. "What's wrong, Sarah?"

Sarah began to cry and Tommy tried manfully to hold back his tears. At the house, Duchess scratched the closed door again and barked once. McKendree dropped the reins and strode to the house. He reached the door as it opened. A grim-faced Charles Goodwin blocked his entrance.

McKendree saw the deep lines that etched Goodwin's face, the look of immense emotion in his friend's eyes. Like the children, he too had been crying. His heart moved up into his throat. He managed to say, "What is wrong, Charles?"

Goodwin shook his head once, almost imperceptibly, and stepped aside.

McKendree pounced through the doorway and drew up short. Rachael looked at him from the bedside where she was gently stroking Noreen's pale forehead. The bandage upon Noreen's temple was scarlet, and her shallow breathing barely stirred the coarse gray material of her dress. He dropped the rifles on the table and went to his knee by the bedside. "What happened to her?" he said.

Rachael looked to Charles. He said, "She was attacked, Josh."

"Attacked?" McKendree's eyes grew hard. "Who attacked her?" he said, his voice suddenly regaining its vigor.

Goodwin held out his hand and showed him the bear claw necklace. "Noreen was clutching this when we found her."

"Ribalt!"

Goodwin dropped the necklace on the table. It landed with a brittle sound that seemed to hang in the suddenly silent air like shattered ice crystals. McKendree spun about and looked at his wife a long moment. He glanced up all at once and looked about the cabin.

"Where is Lucas?" he said, turning on Goodwin.

"Sit down, Josh."

McKendree read the awful truth in Goodwin's tone. "No!" he cried out, not wanting to believe it. His eyes swept the cabin again and came suddenly to a halt on the wool blanket on the floor—and on the moccasined foot that protruded from under it. The ground beneath McKendree's feet heaved. He reached out to steady himself, then went down beside the blanket and pulled it back.

Some time later McKendree returned the blanket to its place and stood. Charles Goodwin stepped back in an involuntary move as a cold fear surfaced from some deep pit in his soul. The man he was looking at was not the man he had called friend for all these years—it was the eyes of an animal he looked into now.

McKendree stepped past him, out the door, and with Duchess at his side, strode blindly into the forest.

EIGHT

IT WAS DARK when McKendree returned to the cabin; a lone rectangle of light in a black wilderness. He went straight to the barn, felt in the darkness for a shovel, then crossed to the house. "How is she?" he asked.

Goodwin looked up, startled at seeing McKendree standing in the doorway. "I didn't hear you come in, Josh," he said. "She is the same."

"It is just as well. At least she doesn't have to know what happened to Lucas yet." He glanced at the blanket on the floor. The foot was now covered and the edges of the blanket tucked neatly in, as if to make it look proper—as proper as was possible under the circumstances. McKendree took a lantern out behind the house and set it on a stump next to the grave he had dug two years before. He drove the shovel into the ground and tossed the dirt to one side.

Charles Goodwin followed him into the darkness. "Can I give you a hand, Josh?"

"Go back in the house, Charles," he said sharply.

Goodwin hesitated, but he turned back anyway.

"Charles."

Goodwin stopped.

"This is something I need to do by myself. Thanks for offering, but go on back inside and help Rachael tend to Noreen. Noreen needs you more than I do."

Goodwin nodded his head, and for the next hour he listened to the spade bite into the earth behind the cabin. Then the sound of it ceased and a few minutes later McKendree appeared at the door. He lowered himself wearily at the table. For a while he stared at his hands. He looked at Noreen. Her breathing was so shallow that she might not have been breathing at all. He moved the chair around by her bedside and took her limp hand into his own strong hands, and held it throughout the night.

With daylight graying the window pane, McKendree put the pale hand gently upon the bed and stood. Rachael stirred at the table where she slept with her head upon her arms. Goodwin dropped his feet off the edge of the bed and stretched stiffly out of the hard, straight-back chair where he had spent the night.

"Any change?" he asked quietly so as not to disturb Rachael.

"No." McKendree looked down at the blanket. "It's time." He picked his son up in his arms and went outside. Goodwin shook his wife awake and grabbed Noreen's Bible from the table by the bed.

McKendree buried his son beside the little daughter who had not lived to see her first birthday. Charles Goodwin said words over the grave from Noreen's Bible. Within half an hour he and Rachael were back inside the house; outside the sound of the spade resumed.

When McKendree returned to the house there was once again life in his gray eyes. He took up his rifle and hunting bag and slid the tomahawk into his belt. From its sheath, McKendree drew out a thin scalping knife and looked at the blade in the morning light. He thrust the short blade back into the sheath, put it into his hunting bag and buckled a foot-long rifleman's knife around his waist.

"Where are you going?" Goodwin asked with a troubled voice.

"Where do you think?" McKendree said, pulling the wide-brimmed beaver hat down over his eyes.

"I'll go with you then." Goodwin reached for his rifle and bag.

McKendree stopped in the doorway where the morning sunlight spilled warm into the house and flashed off the floating dust motes. "I'll go alone, Charles." His harsh reply eased a bit and he said, "I'd be beholdin' if you and Rachael stay with Noreen. I'd be no good to her now, and you two know what to do for her. Take good care of her." He looked at Rachael. "Do what you can. Do the best you can for Noreen, Rachael."

Charles Goodwin watched McKendree stride purposefully into the shadows of the barn and a few minutes later galloped away from the house on the back of his sorrel gelding, with Duchess running along at his side. His long rifle lay across the saddle and the fringe of his hunting shirt rippled in the wind as he turned onto the road.

Puffing like a Mississippi side-wheeler, Ribalt pushed on along the game path that wound through the forest toward the mouth of the river that would eventually empty into the Missouri. Ahead, the land climbed in spectacular palisades above the river, and it was toward these he headed.

Jimmy followed the big man, and watched with amazement, and concern, as his father paused to break a branch here and there, or to purposefully plant a foot in the soft mud where a stream crossed the trace or a seep made the earth soft and black.

They proceeded at a steady, distance-covering gait for three hours before Ribalt suddenly stopped and hunkered by the side of the path to catch his breath. He was a powerful man, but it had been years since he had had to push himself like this. He had a good lead. Just the same, he wanted to put enough distance between him and McKendree so he would have time to set a trap if his boys failed to stop him at the house.

Jimmy sipped water from a stream. They had not spoken since they had left the house and now he was eaten up with curiosity about this sudden journey. "Where we headed, Pa?"

Ribalt nodded his head toward the north and sliced a chaw from a plug of tobacco.

"We going to visit Grandpa?" Jimmy asked, skirting a more direct question which might raise his father's wrath if it was something he didn't wish to talk about.

"Maybe . . . later." He bit down on the plug of tobacco and looked around. They had stopped at the edge of a clearing. The trace they followed cut straight across it. Ribalt debated remaining on it or skirting the open ground under the cover of the trees.

Jimmy fidgeted, anxious for his father to resume the march. Ribalt was apparently not ready to tell him the purpose of this trip so the sooner they arrived at their destination, the sooner he would know what was going on. He looked forward to seeing his grandfather. He enjoyed visiting with the old Shawnee who had raised his mother after her parents had been killed in the War of 1812. Although not related by blood, they called him Grandpa, and Raven Feather was pleased that they did so. But there was another reason Jimmy wanted to visit the Shawnee town now. He recalled the young girls that lived there, and the thought of their lovely, smooth-skin faces and budding womanhood brought a slow grin to his face. They had never much interested him before, but now . . . something was different. Something he felt deep inside him made him both excited and vaguely discontented at the same time. Suddenly his thoughts shifted to Sarah Goodwin. His discontentment rose—and he had no idea why.

In the cool of the trees, Jimmy sliced a chaw of tobacco from his own plug and watched Ribalt scan the clearing. Suddenly the trapper struck a pose.

"What is it?" Jimmy said softly.

Ribalt nodded his head at the thick timber off the side of the trace. They moved a dozen rods in that direction and hunched down behind a deadfall. Ribalt slid his rifle over the top of it and said, "Riders coming."

Jimmy had not heard their approach, but he knew enough not to question his father . . . no one with any sense ever questioned Jacques Ribalt. Jimmy pushed his own rifle up over the decaying tree trunk. He could barely make them out through the intervening trees, and as he strained to see who the riders were, he discovered he was holding his breath. He let it go and tried to adopt the stone-still pose his father held.

One by one the riders entered the clearing and started across. Half naked, they rode without saddles and wore turkey feathers in their black, knotted hair. Jimmy counted eight of them, and as far as he could see, they wore no paint. He counted three extra horses too, burdened with something dark and unrecognizable through the trees. As they drew nearer, his father eased off his hair-trigger set, and he began to breathe more easily.

The Indians moved back into the trees, on their side of the clearing, and Ribalt stood up. They stopped and their weapons came around. Some carried bows and arrows, but for the most part, Jimmy saw that their rifles were new, and equal in quality to their own. Ribalt walked unflinching into the face of their guns. The

Indian on the lead horse lifted his weapon then and a smile moved across his face.

"Ribalt," he said. The other weapons turned away.

"Man Who Snores," Ribalt said, raising his right hand. "What the hell are you doing down in this neck of the woods?"

"Hunting." Man Who Snores pointed his rifle at the pack horses. "Three bear in two days. Good hunting."

"Where'd you get the rifles?"

"U.S. Government. Very good guns. Jackson no longer fights us. He makes trade for meat and land, gives us guns sometimes if we are good Indians and agree to move to the land where the sun sets." Man Who Snores grinned wider to let Ribalt know he didn't think much of Andrew Jackson, or his policy of moving the Shawnee to the Oklahoma Territory. He looked at Jimmy. "Your boy?"

"My oldest."

Man Who Snores nodded his head. "He looks like his mother. I have not seen my cousin's boy in many years. He has grown big. Tell me, Ribalt, what are you doing here?"

"I got me a little trouble comin' up from behind. I'm looking for a suitable place to deal with it."

Man Who Snores rocked back on his animal and considered the wide, bearded face before him. "You want help, Ribalt?"

Ribalt stroked his black mane a moment, then said, "Why don't you light down and we'll talk."

The Indian glanced at the sky through the tree-top canopy and said, "It will be dark soon. We make camp here. Have plenty time to talk."

"We make camp, but not here."

They followed Ribalt to a place he felt was far enough off the trace to be safe and dismounted, built a small fire in a ravine and roasted bear meat. As the land darkened Ribalt revealed to them, and to Jimmy, what had occurred, and how he planned to handle it.

The next morning, Ribalt, Jimmy and half the Indians continued north toward the palisades while Man Who Snores took the other three men with him and rode back along Ribalt's trace, looking for a lone rider, and eager to have his blood . . . and his hair.

NINE

THE MORNING was still young, but McKendree felt old, and used up. He tried to recall his aimless trek into the forest the day before, and could not. He remembered only the explosion in his brain that had blinded him for a dozen hours, and then the vast emptiness as he found his way back to the cabin after dark. Now he was numbed, and hollow, and he had only one mission left in life.

His rifle rested heavily in his hand as he rode toward Ribalt's hole-in-the-woods, but it weighed nothing compared to the weight his heart bore. Yet through all his grief, he was aware of a heightened sense of sight and smell, and if he hadn't known better, he'd have sworn there were twice as many birds singing in the tree tops as there had been only two days before. He was thankful for the keenness of his senses. Ribalt was a clever woodsman; an enemy built like a slab of granite, and wrathy as a spring grizzly with cub.

The big yellow dog kept pace with him, sometimes running ahead, but never beyond McKendree's sight, and always returning instantly to his side at the sound of his whistle. As he rode, he thought of Noreen struggling for life, and immediately put that thought far away. His eyes had begun to sting, and he could not afford that kind of distraction. Through the trees ahead, the ground opened up and the squat shape of Ribalt's cabin became visible. McKendree felt a rush of blood to his neck and face, and drew rein as he weighed his next move.

Antoine had never known his father to exaggerate when it came to danger—he'd never known his father to say much about anything

—he decided, growing hot and bored and tired of swatting flies where he sat atop the high platform in the branches of the elm tree. Jacques Ribalt was a man of action, not words. Sometimes Antoine felt that his father might get along better with folks if he for once did use words instead of fists and knives. But that was not Jacques Ribalt's way.

Antoine drew in a breath and let it out in a long sigh. He wondered if his father's parting words of warning had contained more fantasy than fact. He'd spent all of the previous day up this damned tree hugging a rifle and shooing away flies, and it was beginning to look like this morning was shaping up to be more of the same.

He glanced down through the branches and thought of his mother in the house below. What kept her with his father? he wondered. They were so different. Where she tended Antoine's cuts and bruises, and held him tightly when he was frightened, Jacques would pull away from his pain and growl in disgust at his tears. When his father spoke, which was seldom, his words cut into his heart like a knife. When she spoke, it was a salve to heal the injury done by his father.

Antoine shifted uncomfortably upon the little platform and shuffled the rifle into his other arm. It was all so useless, he was certain. He considered climbing down, but a cold fear took hold of him at the thought of his father returning and not finding him at his post. . . .

Movement in the woods caught his eye. He stiffened and leaned forward to peer through the tree branches and leaves. There it was again. A rider obscured by the trees but moving toward the house. Antoine pushed the rifle through the branches and snugged it up against his shoulder, squinting along the barrel. His pulse raced and his forehead broke out in sweat. He had never shot at a man before, he didn't want to now—but his father had said. . . . He tried not to think of the consequences if he failed in this and concentrated only on the shape moving through the trees, beyond the sights of his rifle. His hands were sticky as his fingertip touched the trigger and began to tighten.

The rider stopped then and seemed to blend in with the background. Antoine waited for a clear target, hardly breathing, wishing his father would return to take this responsibility out of his hands.

His target remained motionless. What was he doing out there? Antoine wanted to call down to the house, but dared not for fear of alerting the man waiting just beyond his reach. The horse moved again. Antoine sucked in a breath, held it, tracked the target and as it stepped into the open his finger touched the trigger again.

The horse walked into the clearing, stopped and shifted from one foot to the other beneath the weight of an empty saddle. In a moment of doubt, Antoine looked again at the riderless horse and knew at once what had happened.

McKendree parted the curtains at the back of the cabin with the barrel of his rifle, looked inside and lifted a long leg over the window sill, folding himself silently through the opening with the fluid movement of a cat. He backed against the wall and listened to the shuffling sounds coming from the next room. He looked around the tiny room at the neatly made-up bed and the single chest of drawers. On the wall hung a rippled mirror, and in it his own severe visage stared back at him. He stepped to the door and peered around it.

Louis sat by the table, resewing the seams of a pair of worn-out moccasins. McKendree's view moved to Yellow Leaf, whose back was turned to him as she husked corn in the morning sunlight through the window. The door to the outside was open. From his angle he could see nothing that lay beyond it. He entered the room so quietly that neither of them knew of his presence until he had made certain Jacques Ribalt was not inside the cabin. He reached out and snatched Louis from his chair by the back of his shirt.

Louis gave a startled cry. McKendree set the boy on the floor and poked the barrel of his rifle into his back. Yellow Leaf turned, dropping an ear of corn. Her black eyes went wide.

"Where is Ribalt?" McKendree said, his voice leaving no doubts as to his intentions.

Yellow Leaf stared at him, at the rifle in her son's back, and saw the fire that burned in McKendree's eyes. "My husband is not here. He has gone away," she said, hating Ribalt for leaving them to McKendree's mercy.

That didn't surprise McKendree. He had half expected not to find him here. "Where is he?" he said.

"The Shawnee town up the river," Yellow Leaf said.

For a moment McKendree wanted to pull the trigger anyway, and then take out his rage on the woman facing him . . . but he could do neither. They were not responsible. He saw the terror in Yellow Leaf's eyes and wondered if Ribalt had seen that same terror on Noreen's face a moment before he drove the butt of his rifle into her head. His rage rose and blinded him for an instant. He reined it back and shoved the boy across the room into his mother's arms.

"Outside," he said, waving them to the door with his rifle. He followed them out and swung his rifle up at the branches of the elm tree. "Tell the boy to drop his gun and climb out of the tree."

"Antoine. Put down the gun. Come down here now." There was a rustle of movement high above and the boy climbed down the wooden rungs nailed into the tree trunk. He jumped the last three feet to the ground and stood by his mother. Antoine towered over his younger brother by at least six inches and McKendree guessed his age to be about thirteen—the same as Lucas. . . .

A gray and white dog wandered into view from behind the barn and sat down on the dusty ground to watch him. Yellow Leaf put an arm around each of her sons and pulled them close. McKendree scanned the yard. "You have another boy. Where is he?"

"He went with my husband."

McKendree considered this. It was reasonable. "When did they leave?"

"Yesterday. In the afternoon."

"That would have been just about right," he said, more to himself than to the woman and children watching. He glanced at the youngest boy. "Bring my horse here." McKendree gave a whistle and Duchess trotted into the open. She stopped to give the gray dog a long, hard look. It stood slowly, stretched back its hind leg and cowered back to the barn with its tail between its legs. Duchess went to McKendree's side.

Louis gathered up the reins of the gelding and brought it over. McKendree stepped up into the saddle and looked down at the three of them standing there. "Did Ribalt tell you what this was about?"

Yellow Leaf nodded her head.

McKendree pursed his lips in thought. There was nothing he

could do here. If he'd been a different sort of man he might have taken out his revenge on these three. But he could not take innocent blood. Angry at himself for his weakness, he turned his horse away and started back into the forest.

"McKendree," Yellow Leaf said.

He reined in and looked back. She left the boys standing by the house and came to him. Quickly he brushed at his eyes and pulled himself ramrod straight in the saddle. Yellow Leaf said, "I am sorry for what my husband has done."

McKendree stared at her a moment, then nodded his head. "So am I," he said. He dug his heels into the horse and rode away.

TEN

McKENDREE STRUCK UPON Ribalt's tracks almost immediately and hunkered down beside an animal run to trace the outline of a human foot clad in buckskin with his finger. He swung back up on his horse and started ahead slowly, reading the signs that plainly marked Ribalt's passage through the forest. Once Duchess got hold of the idea, she put her nose to the ground and ranged far ahead of him, turning back occasionally to make certain he was still there.

Morning merged with afternoon; shadows advanced across the forest floor. Overhead, the sky lost some of its intense blue as a thin sheet of gray moved in from the north. The sky darkened and a wind began to rustle the leaves above him.

A few miles farther on, McKendree reined in abruptly to ponder the tracks he was following. Suspicion wrinkled his brow. Duchess came trotting back and sat down. "You stay alert, girl," he said, straining ahead to where the trees closed in. "I'm getting an itch I can't quite reach."

Duchess loped ahead and McKendree redoubled his caution. He smelled the change in the weather and began to scout out a place to spend the night, but the rains came upon him all at once, in violent, slanting sheets, and he was soaked to the skin in minutes. Through the curtain of water he saw the dark entrance to a cave in the broken limestone cliffs and turned his horse toward it.

His horse balked. "Easy, boy," he said, swinging to the ground and leading the animal inside. The ground beneath his feet seemed level enough, though it took a moment for his eyes to divide the dirt from shadow. The horse tugged at its reins. "Easy," McKendree said again, reaching for the animal's flaring nostrils with a gentle hand. "What's got you spooked, boy?"

He peered into the blackness at the back of the cave with little reward, smelled the cool dampness of the place and thought he heard the flutter of wings overhead. "We've got us some bats, that's all," he said in an easy voice. Duchess came in from the rain and sat just inside the drip line, a silhouette against the brighter light outside where the driving torrents beat the dirt into mud.

"Come here, girl."

The dog stood slowly and drew her tail, but remained steadfastly at the entrance. The horse was one thing, but Duchess too? McKendree's fingers tightened around his rifle. He looked back into the blackness. The dog growled. The horse suddenly reared, kicking out, and the reins burned through his palms as the animal spun on its hooves and bolted out of the cave.

He watched his horse disappear into the gray sheets of water. Duchess growled again, pacing, and now from the belly of the cave came a different sound. McKendree spun about to face this unknown danger, and at the same time slowly backed toward the arch of light at the mouth of the cave.

A black shape separated itself from the blackness surrounding him. It reared up on its hind legs and roared. In the gray light its teeth glistened like huge, curved daggers. McKendree turned, caught his toe under a snag and fell. He managed to hold on to his rifle and swung around in time to see the black bear drop back to all fours. Its bulk obscured everything else from his vision. Not taking an extra second to aim, he thrust the rifle barrel against the thick fur and pulled the trigger.

The hammer came down on the frizzen, giving forth a shower of sparks, but that was all. The rain had reached the powder in the pan —the gun was useless. McKendree heaved back on the hammer and tried again, then the bear was on top of him. He reached for the long knife on his belt, feeling her hot breath against his neck and nearly suffocating against the odor of wet fur. But he had fallen on the knife and could not get his hand back to it.

Her roar shook the cave. McKendree grabbed a handful of fur when all at once from the mouth of the cave a yellow-furred rocket exploded and hurled herself through the air. Duchess latched onto the giant creature, instantly changing the course of the attack. The bear reared up, carrying Duchess aloft, turned to this new challenge.

While the battle raged about him in the dim half-light, McKendree brushed the damp powder from the pan, pouring in a fresh prime and thumbing back the heavy hammer. The shot ripped apart the darkness and three feet of flame leaped from the muzzle at the bear. The bullet missed her vitals and she flung off the dog, turning back to McKendree. Now with a bullet in her flank that burned like a red-hot poker, she bounded at him with fury in her wide brown eyes.

McKendree swung his rifle. She knocked it aside. A swipe from one of her paws sent him reeling back against the damp wall of the cave. He shook his head clear, and yanked his long knife free. Putting all his strength behind it, he thrust out, feeling the blade skitter harmlessly off the beast's ribs. She knocked the knife from his fist as easily as she had the rifle.

Her great curved claws raked the side of his arm, shredding the sleeve of his hunting shirt and ripping into his flesh. He tumbled to the ground and the bear moved between him and the gray light at the mouth of the cave, for the first time revealing her full size. At the rear of the cave, McKendree thought he heard the whimpering of a hurt animal. He put his concern for the dog out of mind, focusing his full attention on the bear. In the half-light, she dropped back to all fours and advanced.

Backpedaling, McKendree pushed himself deeper into the cave, all the while struggling to loosen the tomahawk from his belt. It came free a moment before the bear charged. He took deadly aim and swung at a spot behind the ear, putting every ounce of strength he had into the blow. The bear gave forth a tremendous earthshaking roar, reared back and died, collapsing to the ground.

McKendree sat staring at the mound of fur, then he fell back, heaving in huge, searing quantities of air. His wound was beginning to send sharp needles up his arm. He lay there a few minutes with his arm across his eyes, and was startled at the touch of a wet tongue against his cheek.

"Duchess!" he said, levering himself up on one elbow. "You're all right!" He scratched her behind the ears and got painfully to his feet. Duchess followed him with a limping gait outside, where he lifted his face to the rain and let the coolness of it wash away the grime and flush the blood from his arm. He stripped off his shirt, examined the wound, let the rain wash it clean. The four parallel gashes weren't deep, but they pained him mightily, and for a while they took his mind off the pain in his heart that no amount of doctoring could heal.

Afterward, he dabbed the wounds and wrapped them in a clean cloth that Noreen always made him carry when he went hunting. He focused his attention on the job of doctoring, to keep his mind from turning back to more painful thoughts.

When he'd finished, he looked Duchess over and found her uninjured. He turned to the bear lying in the back of the cave, worked the tomahawk from her skull, skinned a portion and cut out a thick roast. The floor of the cave was littered with dry tinder and in a few minutes he had a fire burning, and fresh meat cooking.

The rains continued into the night. McKendree cleaned and reloaded his rifle and then settled down by the fire where its light danced over his stern face as he stared into the nothingness beyond the rain, thinking. Occasionally he'd step to the mouth of the cave and call for his horse. But the animal was gone, putting him afoot. He hauled in damp wood, dried it by the fire and fed it into the flames. His arms stung, but not unbearably so. He roasted more meat to carry with him in the morning, made himself comfortable, and with the big yellow head resting on his lap, went to sleep.

The rains ended some hours later. In the middle of the night a sound dragged McKendree from a deep sleep. When he came full awake he discovered Duchess was no longer by his side. She stood at the entrance to the cave, peering out into a clear night. Stars had replaced clouds, and a large moon cast chalky light over the dark landscape. Her tail was drawn up between her legs and her ears flattened against her head. It was her growling that had awakened him.

ELEVEN

McKENDREE GRABBED UP his rifle as he moved alongside the dog. He glanced at the coals glowing in the fire ring and stopped, dead still in the shadow of the overhang. "Something moving around out there?" he said softly, his suspicions being another bear was eyeing this cave as a nice place to bed down. Duchess continued her low growl and McKendree said, "Well, girl, we won't let this one get within scrapping distance. One bear fight a night is about all I care for."

A shadow moved in the trees, beyond the rubble at the mouth of the cave. McKendree shouldered the rifle and steadied his sights on the spot where he thought his target lay hidden.

Then a voice called to him. "Yo! You there in the cave!"

McKendree had been thinking it another bear. The sound of a human voice made his brain switch mounts. What was a man doing out here moving around in the middle of the night? McKendree tightened his grip on the rifle and was about to reply when the voice said, "You there in the cave. You hear me?"

"I hear you. What is it you want?" The shadow in the woods had stopped moving.

"Smelled your fire. I'd surely appreciate someplace warm to dry off and to light down for the night," the voice said. "I ain't eaten nothing for about a day neither. Mind if I come forward?"

"How many of you are there?"

"Jest me, mister. I ain't even got a dog like that there rangy critter sittin' with you."

"Come on, then, slowly. Stop where I can see you."

A man mounted on a horse separated from the trees and stopped in the moonlight. The rider wore a wide, floppy hat, buckskin leggings and a beaded shirt. He rode a long-legged horse that showed more rib than meat. McKendree stood up, remaining in the shadow of the cave, his rifle pointed. "What's your name?"

"Winfield. George Winfield from Tennessee. And you?"

"Josiah McKendree." Winfield carried a rifle across his lap, and sat his animal in the bone-weary manner of a man who had seen too many days in the saddle. "What are you doing out this late?"

Winfield smiled amiably and said, "Traveling. Can I come forward?"

McKendree judged him to be what he claimed and put up his rifle. "Come on in, Winfield, and welcome." He dropped a hand to Duchess. "It's all right, girl." She stopped growling, but her ears remained flattened. He was growing to appreciate the dog more and more.

Winfield rode over and climbed off his horse. The animal snorted and scrambled back a step. McKendree said, "There's the smell of bear about this place. Best stake her out or she's liable to run off like mine did."

He tied the horse to a tree, and walked as he rode, tired, and sore. Even off the animal, his legs looked like they hadn't got the message. He stepped into the cave and offered his hand. McKendree took it. "I got some bear meat. Stir up that fire and get yourself dried."

Winfield set his rifle aside, hunched down by Duchess and offered the back of his hand. She gave it a superficial smell, as McKendree figured was any dog's obligation to such a peace gesture, and went back inside and lay down. "Nice dog," Winfield said, standing.

"Yep. There's some ready wood over there. I'll fetch some more so's we can dry it."

They built the fire into a roaring blaze that illuminated all the way to the back of the cave. Winfield studied the bear on the floor there, then stripped off his shirt and hung it on sticks near the flames. They cooked more of the bear. Winfield sat back wearily against the wall of the cave with a hunk of meat and his knife, and jabbed a thumb over his shoulder at the carcass.

"How'd you manage that?"

McKendree grinned at the memory of it now and said, "The hard way." He patted the tomahawk at his side.

Winfield whistled and studied the bandages around McKendree's arm. "Looks like she got in a lick too. I hear'd that old David Crockett takes them down that way. I'd personally rather use my gun, or not do it at all."

McKendree grunted and said, "Since they elected him to Congress, Mr. Crockett has been boasting widely about his bear-hunting days."

Winfield laughed. "Well, I reckon getting elected to government can ruin the best of 'em." He carved off a bit of meat and tossed it to Duchess.

"Where you traveling to in such a dogged way, Winfield?"

"To a job," he said, "and maybe see me some of the West before I die. I ain't a young man anymore, McKendree. Turned forty-two last April." He reached into his hunting bag and took out a leather case and a piece of paper. From the case, Winfield carefully extracted a pair of wire-rimmed spectacles, fitted them on his nose and hooked them over his ears. He unrolled the piece of paper, held it near to the firelight and soundlessly moved his lips as he read it to himself as if to reconfirm its contents. He looked up. "You know how to read, McKendree?"

"I do a fair job when I try."

Winfield handed him the paper. McKendree turned it to the fire. It was an advertisement from the *Missouri Republican:*

Wanted: Men with a spirit of adventure to explore the Great Western Wilderness. Colonel William T. MacNamarra is organizing the MacNamarra Company, at Independence, Missouri, for the purpose of trapping beaver, trading goods to the Western Savages, and exploration. Looking for 100 hardy men with no family ties. Must be healthy, have own gun, and horse. The MacNamarra Company will post no bonds. Men selected to explore the Great Western Wilderness will be paid a percentage of Company profits. No guarantees other than honest adventure and danger. All interested, apply on or before October 25, 1829, to Samuel E. Evanston, agent. Grand Waters Hotel, Independence, Missouri.

"You figurin' on joining up with this here Colonel MacNamarra?"

"Yep. I reckon it's the onlyest way I'm a gonna get to see that 'Great Western Wilderness' he writes about—leastwise at my age. I ain't got family ties, and I do have a gun and a horse. How 'bout you, McKendree? You got family?"

McKendree gave Winfield a look that made his blood turn to ice. He had had family ties, strong ties . . . two days ago. Now there was just Noreen, and he couldn't be sure she was still his. Winfield backed away from the question and figured it was a subject best not pursued.

McKendree handed him back the newspaper clipping and winced at the pain that shot through his arm. He said, "That date is still well over a month away, and Independence isn't all that far. Pushing mighty hard, aren't you?"

Winfield folded the paper back into his hunting bag. "Like I said, I ain't so young anymore. I figure if I wait until the last minute some young buck gonna take my place. I ain't had nothing much important to work at these last few years, 'cept trapping and stayin' out of the Injuns' way, and I figure I ain't got a whole lot of time left to rest on my haunches." Winfield nodded his head at McKendree's arm. "Looks to me like that bear hurt you some."

"It'll heal."

"I got some salve in my kit that'll do you good. I'll get it." He stood stiffly, walked to his horse and came back with a tin can in his hand. "Let me take a look."

McKendree relented and unwrapped the bandages. Winfield frowned. "She caught you good. Not deep, though." He spread on the thick cream. At first it stung like a swarm of bees, but in a moment warmth spread up to his shoulder and numbed the pain.

"That's good stuff," he said after he'd wrapped the wound.

"An Injun friend back in Tennessee brews this up. Don't know what's in it, but it works." Winfield tossed him the tin. "Here, you keep this one. I got another in my kit."

McKendree looked at the tin, then handed it back to Winfield. "Thanks, but you're gonna want it where you're going."

Winfield shook his head and pushed it away. "I got all I need, and they last a long time, anyway. Keep it in exchange for the bear meat. Besides, you might need it where you're headed."

McKendree looked at him suspiciously. "How do you know where I'm heading?"

"I don't—not exactly, but I can see in your eyes you got a demon wrestling inside you, and I'll wager there's gonna be some blood shed before you're set free of him."

McKendree turned the tin over in his hand. It was a demon for certain that drove him on, but it was the devil himself he was after. "Thanks." He put it into his hunting bag and took out his clay pipe and tobacco.

Winfield loaded up a pipe too and the men sat by the fire, smoking. In a little while Winfield knocked the ashes from his bowl and said, "Sometimes it helps to talk—just to settle things right in the brain, you know."

McKendree thought this over while Winfield packed in another bowl and touched a firebrand to it. He stood and leaned against the mouth of the cave, looking at the moon—full and ripe—a blanched melon resting almost atop the trees of the forest at this late hour. He had harbored his anger and grief to himself all day and now suddenly he needed to tell someone about it . . . and here was Winfield; a stranger out of the night who wanted to listen. He looked up at the stars that brightened the heavens, and didn't understand the God that Noreen and Reverend Daub worshipped. What kind of God allows men like Ribalt to live and takes away innocent children? He frowned at the thought. The same kind of God that sends wayward strangers to listen to a grief-stricken man's troubles.

He turned slowly from the night and peered at the man sitting by the fire. He remembered a passage Noreen had once read to him from her Bible. He tried to recall the words exactly but could only come up with something that sounded like *entertain strangers, for you may be entertaining angels unawares.* He grinned at the thought. He returned to the fire, and told Winfield about Lucas, and Noreen . . . and about Ribalt.

TWELVE

McKENDREE FINISHED his story and Winfield sat staring into the dying flames, stirring at the embers around the edges of the fire with a spindly stick. "It's a burden to bear," he finally said in a thoughtful voice, "and I don't know as I'd handle it any different than you are." He pulled the brand from the fire and watched the flame shrink and go out, leaving only the tip glowing red. "I wish you luck, but after it's over, you're still gonna have an ache right here that ain't gonna go away." He touched his beaded buckskin shirt above his heart.

McKendree knew that. Killing Ribalt could never ease the pain of losing Lucas, or pay for his and Noreen's suffering. But knowing that didn't make the job ahead any less urgent.

"I know," he said, sucking thoughtfully at the stem of his pipe. The flames of the campfire reflected off his wide, staring eyes. To the east the sky was growing faintly pink. He'd spent the night talking, and he felt some of the weight he'd been carrying around ease off his heart. He glanced at the sky and said, "I wish I'd thought to bring some coffee."

"Coffee?" Winfield grunted as he got to his feet. His joints ached and he stretched a leg back like a tired old dog. "I got me some in my kit," he said. "I'll fetch it."

Duchess lifted her head and watched Winfield walk stiff-legged out to his horse. He came back with a sack and a blackened pot. McKendree gathered wood, thankful for the distraction of the task —and for Winfield's timely arrival. He regretted they'd have to part company, but Winfield had his job ahead of him . . . and so did McKendree.

They brewed coffee, ate a breakfast of bear meat and wild raspberries, then broke up the fire. Winfield tightened up his saddle while McKendree packed some meat for him to carry. As the sun climbed above the tree tops, Winfield lifted himself atop his horse.

"I don't reckon we'll ever cross traces again, McKendree," he said, settling his rifle across his lap and squinting at the new morning, "but if we ever do, I'll be real curious to hear how all this turns out." He offered his hand. McKendree took it.

"You take care, Winfield."

Winfield smiled thinly. "I'm good at that. You see that you do the same." He turned his horse toward the trees, paused to throw a final wave, and then he was gone.

McKendree returned to the cave for his rifle and hunting bag, and threw a sack of meat over his shoulder. Duchess was eager to be off, and she bounded ahead of him. It would be slow going now, afoot, but it didn't matter. Ribalt was afoot too, and the distance between them had narrowed considerably. He felt more at ease with himself. Considering Winfield's timely arrival, he wondered fleetingly if angels really didn't visit men.

Then a footprint, not quite washed away by the rains, appeared in the soft earth—and another, and all at once his concentration was riveted upon Ribalt's trace. The burning urgency returned, and there was no place for fanciful diversions.

Jimmy Ribalt leaned against a decaying stump, eating a breakfast of opossum meat and sipping stout black coffee. He was unaware that his father had stopped behind him, watching him as an eagle might a scurrying rodent a moment before starting its dive. Jacques Ribalt glanced around the campsite, at the Indians hunched about the small fire, then back to his son. He could see something was on the boy's mind. He took little interest in his children's problems, but if there was any room in his cold heart for a child, Jimmy was the closest there came to filling it.

"Got something stuck in your craw, boy?"

The sudden rumble of his father's voice from behind him made Jimmy leap about, spilling coffee onto his legs.

Ribalt's coal-black beard rustled apart as a thin grin appeared. It might have reflected humor, or just a sneer. Jimmy said, "You sure did give me a start, Pa."

Ribalt stepped over the deadfall and sat down. "It's about time you begin paying attention to who is coming up on your back side."

Embarrassed, Jimmy glanced down where his breakfast had landed on the ground. He brushed ineffectually at the coffee stains on his pants.

"Sit back down," Ribalt said. "You got something troubling you?"

Jimmy found himself sitting back against the stump. It was always like that. You simply obeyed Ribalt—or you paid for it at the back of his massive hand. He said, "There ain't nothing bothering me, Pa."

"You're lying."

Jimmy looked away and felt his cheeks warm. "I was only thinking, Pa."

"About what?"

How could he tell him? He marshaled his courage and said, "I was thinking about girls."

Ribalt's rumbling laugh filled the clearing. It turned the heads of the Indians by the fire and caused Jimmy's reddening face to instantly burn scarlet. Jimmy looked at his father sharply. Ribalt's black eyes glistened with humor and he said, "Ease back, boy. I reckon when I was your age I mostly thought of gals too. There are plenty of gals at the Shawnee town. When we get there we'll fix you up with one of 'em."

"I ain't interested in those girls, Pa."

"They're as good as any you'll find," Ribalt said, suddenly impatient with the boy. "Your ma is Shawnee, and so was my ma."

"I know. It ain't nothing again' the Shawnee . . . it's just that . . ." He hesitated.

"You've found another little gal to turn your head, ain't you, boy. It's that farmer's little girl, Sarah."

Jimmy showed open surprise. Ribalt frowned and said, "Don't think I ain't seen the way you've been keeping an eye out on the Goodwin place. And I can't say as I approve. I was hoping when you picked a woman, it would be one of your own kind. Boy, you're more Shawnee than white, and what ain't Indian is French. Damn!

You've no place with a pale-faced Englander, and I think you need to ponder that awhile."

"But I like her, Pa. She's pretty, and her voice is soft, and her eyes are blue—"

"Blue!" Ribalt laughed. "Look in the mirror, boy. Your eyes are black, black as pitch."

Jimmy's hackles rose. It angered him that his father wasn't giving him the right to choose in this matter. He said, "I remember Grandpa, before he died. His eyes were blue!"

"It was some of that damned English blood what crept in when my great-grandpa took a Herefordshire milkmaid for a walk out to the barn one night," he said. "We've purged that from our family and I don't much care for you to bring more of it back into it." He stopped, thought a moment, then said, "But the decision is up to you, boy. As far as picking a woman goes, I've spoke my piece. You pick the one that pleases you and we'll make her fit the family right enough."

Jimmy hardly believed what he heard. Was that all he was going to say on the matter? He didn't believe the man would relent so easily. To test the waters he said, "Then if it's my decision, I've made it. I want Sarah Goodwin."

Ribalt snorted and stood up. He looked down at the boy, then nodded his head. "All right, if'n that's what you want, that's what you'll get. After I take care of McKendree, and after we stop to see the folks at the Shawnee town, and you get a good look at the offerings there, and you still want that scrawny English gal, then I'll get her for you."

Ribalt called to the Indians. It was time to leave. The Shawnee packed their horses. Ribalt and Jimmy, still afoot, struck out north toward the palisades along the river where he planned his ambush. From there it would be a short trip to the Shawnee town, and Ribalt figured he'd find plenty of reasons there to change the boy's mind about Sarah Goodwin.

Many miles to the south, Man Who Snores and his companions had found a rock overhang to huddle under from the rains, but not until they had been soaked clear through. Now, not wanting to light a fire and attract attention, they decided an early start was the easiest and quickest way to dry out. Ribalt had given Man Who Snores a description of McKendree, but to the Indian, one white frontiersman on horseback pretty much looked like another. . . .

So, when he saw the flickering movement through the trees, he determined at once it could only be the very same man that they were hunting. He and his companions moved silently under cover until they had positioned themselves ahead of and above the rider—a lone man on horseback. Man Who Snores knew he had found the one pursuing Ribalt. The one called McKendree.

The white man looked older than he had imagined, and more tired, and the horse he rode had seen better years, but that only made Man Who Snores' task that much easier. The morning was but a few hours old when Man Who Snores struck with swift viciousness. The rider barely had a moment to swing his rifle off his lap when the first arrow whistled through the air and drove deep into his shoulder.

The man fired. One of the Indians tumbled from the moss-covered rocks where the arrow had come from. He gritted his teeth against the pain of the arrow in his shoulder and leaped to the ground, scrambling for cover. A second arrow embedded itself in his thigh as he lunged forward. He stumbled, drawing his knife free of its scabbard even as he fell. A third arrow whistled through the air. It dug into his side, but he had cover within reach . . . then a rifle shot rang out.

The bullet pierced his heart and he died instantly.

Man Who Snores stood up upon the rocks and raised the rifle in victory above his head. He climbed down, stooped over the fallen warrior and saw that he was dead. Gray Dog peered down soberly. Man Who Snores lifted the white man's hair—what little there was of it—and decided it was not much of a prize. He would present it to Ribalt. He went through the man's belongings, taking his rifle, knife and horse. Then they tied their dead companion across his horse and headed back to the appointed meeting place. It was not yet seven o'clock in the morning.

In another part of the forest McKendree too was heading toward that rendezvous.

THIRTEEN

CHARLES GOODWIN was in the barn fetching a spade when he heard the pounding of hooves in the yard. He stuck his head outside to see McKendree's horse standing between him and the house, its nostrils flaring and a wild look in its eyes. Goodwin leaned the shovel against the barn and walked slowly to the animal.

"Easy, boy," he said, reaching for the reins that hung to the ground. The gelding backed up, rolled its eyes. Goodwin got hold of the reins and turned them once around the porch railing. "What's gone wrong, boy?" he said, stroking the sorrel's sweating neck. "Where is Josh?"

"What is it, Charles?" Rachael said, stepping out the door. Her face wore a tired, sad look, and a heavy weariness stooped her shoulders, but she drew herself up straight when she saw the horse, for she understood what it meant.

"Reckon I ought to go looking for him?"

Rachael shook her head slowly, pulling her eyes off the horse. "No," she said quietly. "If you had any idea where to look . . ."

"He has to be at Ribalt's place, Rachael."

"I don't want you going, Charles," she said, surprised at the emotion that had burst forth with her words. She swallowed heavily and said, "I don't want you, or ours, to end up like the McKendrees."

"I can't stand by and do nothing, Rachael."

"I know," she said. Suddenly there were tears in her eyes and she turned abruptly back into the cabin. Charles stood there a moment, not certain of his next move. He took the horse to the barn, where he unsaddled it and forked hay into its stall.

He stepped out to study the field of corn McKendree had planted. It was ripe and ready to be harvested. There was the stock that needed tending too. Suddenly Charles Goodwin had the responsibility of two places to run . . . and he was only one man.

He drew in a deep breath and let it out slowly. Perhaps he ought to let the place go. . . . In a year the fields would be overgrown, in two, young saplings would be nudging up against the cabin. But there was still a chance McKendree might return, as slim as that chance looked at the moment. Return to what? he thought bitterly.

Goodwin had to get back to his own place soon, back to his own chores. He ought to ride into St. Elizabeth and report all that had been happening to the law. That was the proper course to take now, considering the circumstances. The law ought to be the one to go after Ribalt, not him.

He remembered sadly what had brought him to the barn in the first place. Glancing back to the shovel resting against the wall, he sighed wearily, snatched it up and went out behind the house.

Josiah McKendree came to a sudden halt and remained as still as the surrounding trees. Indians had all at once come into view. Cautiously, he lowered his hand to Duchess and whispered, "Stay, girl."

With the natural instincts of a hunter, the big dog knew what was required of her. She flattened her ears against her head and deep within her throat came a low growl that McKendree alone could hear. But she did not move, she did not bark.

McKendree counted three riders, and upon closer study, he determined that a fourth Indian rode belly down. They moved out of the trees, onto the trace that he had been following, and then abruptly altered their course to follow it, not fifty feet ahead of where he lay in hiding. There was a fifth horse with them, different from the Indian ponies. Larger, but with less meat on its bony frame. It was an old horse, and it wore a saddle instead of only a blanket, and . . .

"Winfield!" he said to himself. He tried not to speculate on his fate, but knew full well there could be only one explanation for his horse now being among these Indians. McKendree waited for the Shawnee to ride ahead. He left cover and stooped over their tracks, and glanced up the trace they had left in their passage. Moving into an easy, distance-covering dog trot, he followed it back.

In an hour he reached the clearing and stopped just short of it. He waited, but there was nothing left here that could harm him. Duchess moved out ahead of him and trotted to the bloodied body lying upon the grass. McKendree had experienced too much sadness these last days to feel any more of it at the sight of Winfield's scalped and stripped body. His belongings were scattered about, wind-blown upon the grass, and caught in shrubbery. He could not feel the sadness that should be there. Instead, an intense anger boiled up inside him.

He knelt down beside the frontiersman and touched the beaded shirt that had been ripped open. Then he saw something fluttering upon the ground. He caught it, and turned it over in his hands.

Men with a spirit of adventure to explore the Great Western Wilderness, it started.

McKendree gave a short, bitter laugh. "Well, Winfield, I reckon we did meet up again, but not the way either you or I figured. Fate has a way of toying with men's lives like that. I regret you ain't gonna get to see that Great Western Wilderness. If I ever make it out that way, I'll take a gander at it for you." This man had been no angel, but he had been a friend, and that had to account for something. He promised himself that if he ran across the Indians that did this, he'd avenge Winfield's death. It occurred to McKendree that he was tallying up quite a list of avenging.

McKendree tucked the newspaper into his linsey-woolsey shirt pocket and headed back into the forest. Within half an hour he was once again on Ribalt's trace, and to his pleasure, the murdering Shawnee were heading in the same direction.

Man Who Snores read the signs of Ribalt's passage through the forest with the same clarity a literate man might find in the written word. He understood Ribalt's reasons for laying down such a plain, obvious trace, but he also knew, with some pride, that now it was unnecessary. He carried McKendree's scalp with him. Gray Dog led the pony carrying Broken Nose and Elk Rider held the reins to Winfield's horse as they climbed the rising ground in single file.

All around them, the Missouri palisades cut wild and beautiful sculptures in the land. Layers of moss-covered rocks, stacked atop each other like building blocks and exposed by rain and snow and wind, climbed on either side of them, rising dramatically. Eventually, the Indians found themselves atop the cliffs, threading their way along the edge of them, and a hundred feet below, the Missouri River flowed strong and wide, carrying with it rafts of vegetation. A dark, muddy river, bearing the silts of mountain ranges a thousand miles away. Mountains that neither Man Who Snores, Elk Rider, nor Gray Dog ever dreamed existed.

They reached Ribalt's camp by late afternoon and swung off their horses. Ribalt rose from where he was sipping coffee over a small campfire. Jimmy and the other Indians gathered around their horses, examined Broken Nose and asked what had happened.

"McKendree got in a shot," Man Who Snores said. "Broken Nose fell to his bullet."

"And what about McKendree?" Ribalt said.

"McKendree is dead," Man Who Snores said, throwing out his chest. He reached back for the scalp tied to his blanket.

Ribalt's face eased into an unaccustomed smile. "Dead? Them's sweet words to my ears, Man Who Snores."

Man Who Snores presented the scalp to him.

Ribalt's smile solidified and his black eyes hardened. "What is this?"

"McKendree's scalp. A gift to you, Ribalt."

Ribalt stared at the balding, graying scrap of flesh and hair, and was suddenly gripped by a quivering shaking that started in his belly and worked its way up until his entire body convulsed like that of a man possessed. They watched this change come over him with deadly silence, like the breathless wind before a storm. Jimmy instantly retreated a good distance off, knowing from experience what was to follow.

Man Who Snores continued to smile, with his hand outstretched, offering the gift, sensing that something was amiss, but not yet grasping the full portent of the change that had overtaken Ribalt.

But the smile vanished, and Man Who Snores seemed to shrink as Ribalt's quivering erupted with volcanic consequences.

"You red fool!" Ribalt roared. "That ain't McKendree!" His words reverberated like thunder through the forest.

"But . . ." Man Who Snores had begun to say when his words were cut short by Ribalt's fist. It crashed into the Indian's face like the flying hoof of a wild stallion and sent him tumbling back a dozen feet. Blood gushed from his crushed nose. He tried to sit up, but fell back. Ribalt stepped over him, lifted him off the ground by his porcupine-quill breastplate and heaved his fist back again.

Before Ribalt could strike another blow, a hand reached out and turned him about. Gray Dog's fist swung wide, clipping Ribalt upon his great, bearded chin. Ribalt took the blow without a backward step and came back with a powerful jab to Gray Dog's belly. The wind went out of him, and Gray Dog staggered back. Ribalt came forward like a humped-back bear and hit him a second time. He picked the smaller man off his feet and heaved him across the clearing as if he had been no more than a gunnysack of potatoes.

Gray Dog crashed into the ground. He groggily pushed himself up, shaking his head. His eyes locked onto Ribalt, afire with hatred. He glanced at a bow and arrow lying a dozen feet away, scrambled to his feet and leaped for them, fitting an arrow to the string as he came about.

Ribalt reached into the top of his moccasin and came up holding a sliver of shiny steel. His arm cocked and the slim knife glinted in the sunlight as it wheeled across the ground that separated the two men. It found its mark, precisely where Ribalt had aimed. Gray Dog's eyes bulged, surprise gaped his mouth open. The arrow slipped from his fingers, sailing harmlessly into the air, and he fell forward, dead.

With the suddenness of a passing storm, Ribalt's fury left him. He blinked, seemingly seeing what had happened for the first time, and looked around at the Indians standing there. Man Who Snores sat upon the ground, holding his nose with blood running through his fingers. Jimmy remained some distance off with his rifle ready. None of the Indians seemed particularly eager to pursue the disagreement any further.

Ribalt strode over to Gray Dog, turned him over with the toe of his moccasin. A spot of blood stained the porcupine breastplate above his heart. The knife had neatly parted the quills there and lay embedded to its hilt. Ribalt yanked the blade free, wiped the blood from it on the Indian's buckskin leggings and returned it to its hidden sheath.

"McKendree still lives. I intend to have that man's scalp. You can help or you can ride away with your tails between your legs. Make up your minds."

Man Who Snores stood and approached him. "Ribalt, I run from no man, not McKendree . . . not you. I will stay until you have this man's blood." He turned to his companions. They nodded their heads and eased off their hair-trigger setting. The storm had passed—for the moment—and in its wake the Indians were left with another man to bury.

A smile slowly eased its way across Ribalt's face. He had what he wanted, allies, and it didn't matter a damn that two men had died for it. "Good. Then let's get cracking. I don't want McKendree to arrive before the trap is baited." He glanced at Gray Dog and Broken Nose. "Get those two underground before they start attracting flies."

Ribalt turned away, then stopped and looked back with the beginnings of a plan forming in his head. "Hold up on that," he said. "I got me a different idea. Maybe we can still get some use out of these two after all. . . ."

FOURTEEN

McKENDREE SMELLED the smoke of their fire a mile off as it came through the moist green ravine that cut between the limestone layers. The tracks that marked their passage were plain enough, even to someone not skilled in reading such things, and to McKendree, they told a story much deeper than simply that a string of horses, and two men on foot, had recently passed through here. It told him something that made the hair at the nape of his neck stand up and brought on that itch he could never quite rid himself of by scratching.

He paused to consider the possibilities, and came to the only conclusion possible. "They're baiting us, girl," he said, stroking the dog's wide head. He studied the rising land, smelled the moistness of earth and decaying leaves. It was the sort of morning McKendree used to find invigorating; the sort of morning where long walks would add meaning to life. Now there was none of that. It was a morning laced with impending death—promising no good.

McKendree shucked this black mood and brought his mind, sharp and clear, back to the problem at hand. He moved off the trace and ate the remainder of his bear meat, throwing a chunk of it to the dog. It was a meager breakfast, and he longed for a cup of Noreen's strong black coffee, but that would have to wait until he had finished this business. He tried not to think of the wife he had left back home, or of the son he had buried, and moved off again, stalking cross-country. He thought instead of Ribalt, and the price the man would pay for the hole he had made in McKendree's life.

Duchess stayed near to him now. Atop the palisades, he reached level ground and moved through the trees until the land fell away in steep, majestic cliffs. The edges of the rocks below were softened by blankets of moss and vines, where white pine clung tenuously, seemingly growing out of the cracks in the limestone. Far below flowed the muddy Missouri River. It was a wide, slow river. Upon it, the low, flat shape of a barge, loaded with trade goods, drifted with the current down toward St. Louis. On another part of the river, a keelboat pushed up against the current, a dozen men on her gunnels poling her along with long wooden staffs.

McKendree backed away from the edge. Their campfire smoke came strongly on the steady wind here above the river. His senses were alive again, as they hadn't been since his younger days, before he had married and settled down. The Shawnee had murdered his family in Tennessee and he had taken out after them. One by one he made them pay for the lives of his family. He had thought that part of his life was behind him, but here he was, thirty-two years old—he might as well have been eighteen again.

He stroked the dog's head. "Stay, girl," he said, moving off. When he looked back Duchess was watching him, waiting to be called, but remaining precisely where McKendree had told her to. He didn't want the dog along now to inadvertently give away his position by an anxious growl or bark. He wanted to scout the situation by himself. "Stay," he reinforced softly and moved off. He knew Ribalt's camp was only a short distance away, and that Ribalt had taken great pains to lead him straight to it.

Silent as the wisp of smoke, he melted among the trees, a ghost in buckskins and linsey-woolsey, moving with the shadows, placing each step as if the ground was brittle ice. McKendree felt a rush of warmth spread through his body as he inched nearer. He stopped. Through the trees ahead lay a clearing. He smelled the green-wood smoke. Green wood! He grinned to himself and figured they couldn't have been more obvious. There was one clear approach to the camp. The one they'd be expecting him to use. The one they'd be watching. To his left were the cliffs. Unscalable. They'd not be expecting him from that direction.

McKendree eased himself over the edge of the palisades. His toe found a slender ledge. He glanced at the brown Missouri far below him. In the distance a keelboat was coming around a bend in the river. He turned his full attention to traversing the treacherous cliff-side unseen, using toeholds and clinging vines. A rock broke beneath his foot and sent a shower of pebbles raining down to make infinitesimal white splashes in the water below him. He hung there, gripping a thick vine in his powerful hand, and heaved himself back up to the toehold. In another minute he pulled himself up safely on the far side of the clearing, near the back side of Ribalt's camp.

McKendree moved closer and dropped to his knees to study the camp. He could clearly see the smoke curling from the green-wood fire. Near it lay one of the Indians, asleep beneath a blanket. McKendree had guessed the Shawnee that had murdered Winfield were in league with Ribalt. Now he knew it for certain. He saw another man sitting against a tree. Ribalt! McKendree eased nearer. There were at least four more men about, but he didn't see any of them. He suspected they'd be looking for him in another part of the forest and he stepped quietly to a nearer tree.

His angle changed and he saw clearly that Ribalt, too, was sleeping. His head leaned forward upon his beaded shirt and a felt hat kept the sun off his face. McKendree figured to move in closer and get the drop on Ribalt, but even as he moved, a warning bell went off somewhere deep in his subconscious. It surfaced to his conscious thoughts and he drew up instantly. Asleep? His right ear had begun to itch. Both of them? Without thinking, McKendree began to backpedal, making a careful retreat to the cliffs.

Something was very wrong here. He put distance between himself and the camp, and when he neared his avenue of escape, stood and turned. . . .

A rifle stared him in the face. Over its long barrel the black eye of a half-naked Indian squinted along the sights.

McKendree sucked in a breath and froze. Out the corner of his eye another figure stepped into view. This second Indian was carrying Winfield's rifle; his face was black and blue, and swollen.

"Take it easy with those smoke poles," McKendree said, setting his rifle aside and raising his hands.

The battered-face Indian jerked his rifle toward the clearing. McKendree stepped into it, stopping to look down at the sleeping Ribalt. The man didn't move. Up close, McKendree saw that it wasn't Ribalt at all, but another man dressed in his shirt and jacket.

He glanced at the Indian asleep by the fire. He didn't move either. He'd been suckered into their trap slicker than a greenhorn at a snipe hunt.

McKendree came about at the sound of laughter. Ribalt stood with his hands on his hips. His head was a fierce tangle of black hair that merged with his beard and spread down his naked chest. He dwarfed the Indians with him. His son, Jimmy, was at his side with a rifle to his shoulder.

"I figured you'd be coming, McKendree," Ribalt said. He strode over to the dead man and removed the hat and shirt. The body fell forward. There was a round, bloodless hole on its back in line with the heart.

McKendree looked at Ribalt with cold hate. He was fully aware of the dangerous situation he was in, but it didn't matter now. All that mattered was thrusting his fingers around Ribalt's neck and squeezing the life out of him.

"You'd like to get ahold of me. I can see it in your eyes, McKendree. I can't say as I blame you."

"Why, Ribalt? Why did you do it?"

The big trapper frowned and shook his head. "It was you I wanted. Your family got in my way."

"Me?"

"My traps. I'd come for my traps. I know'd you took them, and I wanted them back. I still want them back."

"Traps? You murdered my son for some traps?" McKendree advanced toward Ribalt with his fists clenched, but two pairs of hands locked about his arms and pulled him back.

"It ain't the way I planned it, McKendree, but it's done and over, and I still want my traps back."

"Then grow gills, Ribalt, because your damn traps are at the bottom of the river." Someone tugged the tomahawk from his belt and removed the rifleman's knife from its scabbard.

Ribalt's visage blackened. "The bottom of the river!" He struggled to regain control. "Then I guess I ain't got no more use for you." He turned to his son. "Shoot him."

Jimmy glanced at Ribalt, uncertain. "Pa, I ain't sure I want to do that. I mean, kill him like he is, unarmed and all."

Ribalt shifted his view to the boy. "I thought you was different from your brothers, but I see you got your mother's weakness all about you." He snatched the rifle from Jimmy's hands and threw it to his shoulder.

McKendree cast about for some means of escape but the two Shawnee that held his arms meant to keep him. Then, suddenly, a yellow shape hurled itself from the trees and attached itself to the throat of one of the Shawnee holding McKendree. Instantly the man let go. Duchess shook him like a large rat and her tawny coat grew crimson.

In that instant, McKendree threw all his weight at the remaining Shawnee. The crack of a rifle rang out and wood splintered from a tree behind him. He tumbled to the ground, grabbing for the hand holding his long knife. They rolled, each trying to gain an advantage, while Duchess sprang for a scrambling Shawnee who was fitting an arrow to his bow. He dropped the weapon and dove wildly into the forest.

Ribalt hurriedly poured a measure of powder down the barrel of his rifle and thumbed a patched ball into its muzzle.

McKendree and the Indian separated, the Shawnee leaping to his feet. He still had possession of McKendree's knife as the two men circled. McKendree riveted his eyes upon it while a part of his brain watched Ribalt's progress with the rifle. All at once the Indian sprang forward. McKendree dodged left at the last minute and felt the sting of the blade piercing as the knife plunged into hard muscle and skidded along bone.

McKendree staggered back, dropped to his knees. He saw the hilt of the knife protruding from his side, felt its sharp point coming through the back of his shirt. His vision blurred. The Shawnee stepped into his view, grinning, his own knife in his hand this time.

Ribalt finished loading the rifle but there was no need for it now. Man Who Snores stood over McKendree, raising the scalping knife.

McKendree shook his head to clear his vision. He tried to scoot himself back, but consciousness was slipping away. To his swimming brain, he imagined something akin to a golden explosion over his head. An explosion made up of four legs and blood-drenched fur. Man Who Snores gave out a startled cry an instant before his throat was ripped open. Blood spurted as from a fountain and the dog tore into the Indian as if she intended to have his head as a token of her conquest.

McKendree didn't wait to see the outcome. He staggered to his feet, swayed as he tried to hold his balance. Bearing the wrenching pain of the knife through his side, he hobbled to the edge of the palisade, stopped, caught his balance. The waters moved in great swirling currents around the rocks far below. He looked back. Ribalt was raising his rifle. No avenue of escape was left to him, and he leaped out over the edge.

The side of the palisade rushed past him. A flash of green was all he remembered, and below, the rocks and muddy water rose up to meet him.

The River

FIFTEEN

RUDD GUTTERIE stood atop the cabin of the keelboat *Gutt's Bucket,* leaning his weight full onto the rudder as the boat came around the bend in the river. His inattentiveness had brought him too near the shore, and now it loomed, treacherous. The current caught hold of the boat and was sweeping it toward a snag that lifted dead and waterlogged branches like twisted arms. Arms that wanted to reach out and scuttle his little boat.

"Reese, Karl, get some poles on this side!" he shouted, cursing himself for paying more attention to the celebration going on inside the cabin beneath his feet than to the river. The boat heeled over as the broad, flat rudder took a bite out of the river, but the swift current had them now, carrying them toward the snag, and Gutterie wasn't bringing the nose about fast enough!

"Up on the bow! Quickly!" he said as the two men came out the door and saw their captain heaving sideways on the long rudder shaft. They instantly saw the looming disaster and snatched poling staffs from off the pegs. At the forward point, Reese and Karl thrust them into the muddy water and felt the poles sink into the silt at the bottom of the river as they put their muscle into them. Backs bowed and straining, shoulders bunched, knees bent, legs pushing against the rough wooden decking, they grunted, and in slow degrees the bow came about.

Andre LaVoie stepped out of the cabin and staggered along the angling gunnels. It was not the list of the boat that made his steps unsteady, but the whiskey that sloshed in his stomach and warmed his cheeks. As his vision cleared, he recognized the disaster ahead and grabbed another pole, lending his muscle to the task.

The snag swept by, a dozen feet off the *Gutt's Bucket's* port side, as the boat cut across the current. The bottom of the river dropped away until the poles became useless. As his boat moved into deeper water, Gutterie let out a heavy sigh and eased back on the rudder, allowing the current to straighten them out.

"Close one, heh, Rudd?" Reese Sculty said, swinging his dripping pole inboard and putting it back on the pegs that protruded from the wall of the cabin.

"Close one," Rudd said, steering a course into the middle of the river.

"What the hell is a goin' on up there?" a voice shouted from below. "It's raining whiskey in here! Quick, Ben, git me that cup over there. I wanna collect some of this manna from heaven!"

"Just tip your mouth up, Bill," another voice said, sounding near as drunk as the first.

Rudd glanced at the cabin roof beneath his boots and grinned at the whiskey bottle rolling about on its side, spilling amber fluid through the cracks in the roof. He stomped his boot on the roof. "Bring me up another John Barleycorn, Bill Bensen. I done went and spilled this one."

"Yes, sir. Right away, Captain," Bensen called back with playful mockery. "I reckon we got us plenty to go around a time or two."

"We ought to, you ugly river rat. That steamer had her a right fat liquor larder."

Karl grinned up at Gutterie from the deck as he replaced his pole too. "Mighty shame she ran aground like she done. Wonder how her captain could have got himself in such a fix?"

Gutterie laughed. Bensen climbed up with a fresh bottle of whiskey, pulled the cork with his teeth and handed it to Gutterie. "Want me to steer awhile?"

Gutterie cocked an eye at the man and took a long swallow from the bottle. "You're drunk, Bensen. You're liable to run us aground."

"Yes, sir," Bensen said, throwing his hand to his forehead in a salute that would have broken his nose if he'd missed. "Just like Reese done to the side-wheeler *Laurel.*" They all thought that was hilarious. Rudd held tight to the rudder to keep from falling over, partly from laughter, partly from all the whiskey they had slugged down since selling their cargo in Independence—cargo that had originally started for that town in the holds of the *Laurel.*

Rudd Gutterie was an amiable river pirate, both drunk and sober, but drunk, his pocked face turned scarlet and his eyes crossed. His keelboat was one of three that worked the river as a team—like a pack of wolves—raiding unsuspecting shipping, off-loading their cargo, hauling it up the river and selling it where they could. Gutterie was a stocky man, five foot eight inches tall, with a belly that was beginning to strain the buttons of his red shirt. He had a small, round jaw, more often than not covered with gray whiskers, brown hair with wisps of gray running through it, sharp blue eyes and a nose that seemed at first glance to be as wide as his upper lip. A second glance would tell you it had only been broken too many times.

Andre LaVoie said, "I like working steamboats, Rudd. They carry cargo what I'd call pleasing to the taste." He grinned crookedly and went inside for another bottle.

Rudd said, "Trouble with steamboats is they're owned by companies what's gonna come looking for 'em, and they have manifests what tells the authorities exactly what they was carryin'."

Karl said, "We can always haul it off to the cave and sit on it until they stop looking."

Gutterie leaned on the rudder, guiding the boat farther out into the river. "They never stop lookin', Karl," he said, staring across the river to the magnificent palisades that rose from the water's edge. The morning light upon the limestone face seemed to ignite the green of the clinging vegetation with a brilliancy only seen in early morning or late afternoon. Gutterie and his partners had a cave in those cliffs, farther down the river, and that cave was packed solid with the fruits of their labors. He tipped back his bottle, then squinted at the swirling water ahead that marked some submerged obstruction. He swung farther to starboard and the palisades loomed nearer. Gutterie judged the speed of the water and calculated they should be spotting the pier in half an hour. He thought of Emma, and of his daughter, Carlotta. Dinner should be on the table by the time they heaved to and tied up. All he'd eaten since leaving Independence was some venison Reese Sculty had shot along the shore—and the John Barleycorn they had kept back from the raid of the *Laurel.*

Gutterie smacked his cracked lips. Some of Emma's stew and corn bread would go down mighty good about now.

Elliot Soute came along the gunnels, studying the river. "Looks swirly, Rudd. Want I should take some soundings?" Elliot wasn't in any better shape than the other members of Rudd's crew, but he had gone down once in rough water, lost a boat and all her crew, and since then he'd taken it on himself to make certain that it never happened again.

"We've got two fathoms beneath our keel here, Elliot. What you're seeing is a snag caught down there. We're clear."

Elliot grunted, nodded his head, but didn't look convinced. Gutterie said, "Go back and join the others. It's clear all the way down—" He was interrupted by the sound of a rifle shot coming from the direction of the palisades. He and Elliot turned their heads that way.

"Sounds like someone's up there," Elliot said.

"Wonder what he's a shootin' at?" Gutterie said thoughtfully. "Maybe we best put some more water between us and them cliffs, just in case it's us he's a taking potshots at." He swung the bow of his boat to port and took up a brass spyglass.

"See anything, Rudd?"

"Nope. Probably just someone out filling the stew pot." He scanned the rugged cliffs.

"Could be Indians."

Gutterie frowned. "Unlikely it's anything we got to concern ourselves with." He returned his attention to the river.

"Hand me that glass, Rudd." Elliot put it to his eye and focused on something. "There." Elliot pointed, handing the spyglass up to Rudd. "At the edge there. See?"

Gutterie picked out the shape of a man teetering on the edge of the palisades. "Will you look at that!" he said. "That fellow is about to jump!"

"What? Is he simpleminded? A fall like that can kill a man, even if he is lucky enough to miss the rocks."

"He must be, 'cause he sure enough is a gonna jump." He heaved over on the rudder and swung the bow across the current.

"There he goes!" Elliot said.

"The fool," Gutterie murmured. "Reese, Karl, Bill, get up here and put some poles in the water, we're heading in!" Rudd put the spyglass on the falling man a moment before he hit the water. "It looks like he missed the rocks."

"What's that?" Elliot said, pointing. Below them men were scrambling up and grabbing the poles off their pegs.

Peering through the spyglass, Rudd said, "I'll be damned. It's a dog! A big yellow dog, and it's a jumping right after the fellow!"

"What's going on?" Reese asked, thrusting in his pole and finding bottom.

"Some fool just jumped into the river!"

"From up there?"

"That's right," Elliot said. "And there was a dog what jumped after him."

Reese considered the two of them narrowly, and said, "What else you got in that bottle?"

"Shut up and put your back to it," Gutterie barked, not taking his eyes off the place where he'd seen the man hit.

SIXTEEN

THROUGH THE SWIRLING WATER, the *Gutt's Bucket* moved in closer to the limestone cliffs than Rudd Gutterie would have judged prudent had he been even half sober.

"I don't see him nowhere," Reese Sculty said, scanning the rocky shoreline. "The current got hold of him, I'll wager."

Gutterie frowned as he squinted at the rugged ledges at the base of the cliffs.

"Maybe the river washed him down some," LaVoie said.

"Maybe so. Let's ease down a hundred rods and take another look. Keep a sharp eye out for snags and submerged rocks." Gutterie was sobering up fast as he recognized the peril of being so near the palisades in this swift water.

The men poled the boat farther out and let the current carry them down. Elliot Soute caught a glimpse of something half pulled up out of the water on a ledge. "There, Rudd. There he be!"

Rudd peered hard at the rumpled shape and said, "That looks like both of 'em. Heave over and look smart, boys; dancing water about." Using their poles, the crew fended them off the rocks while Rudd maneuvered the *Gutt's Bucket* in close enough for her keel to scrape along the bottom of the river. Gutterie, LaVoie and Bensen jumped into water up to their waist and waded ashore. They stopped abruptly as the big yellow dog by the man's side stood. She flattened her ears and bared her teeth.

"Easy, girl," Rudd said, advancing a step.

The dog barked and arched her back.

"She ain't gonna let you near him, Rudd," Bensen said. "I've seen a dog guard a dead body for more'n a week once. And this fellow sure enough looks dead. Looky, he's got a knife run clear through him. I say we pull out of here and just let it be."

Gutterie whistled softly, feeling the last of the whiskey leave his brain. "He does in fact have a blade run through him. There must of been a hell of a disagreement up there." He glanced up the towering cliffs. "But he don't look dead to me. I can see him still breathing. Come on, girl, we ain't gonna hurt him."

From the boat, Reese Sculty said, "I'm with Bensen. Let him be. He'll only bring us trouble. Besides, that dog ain't gonna give ground, Rudd."

"We're not leaving him, Reese," Gutterie shot back.

"Then let me shoot the dog." Reese turned to Elliot Soute and said, "Get me a rifle from the cabin."

Gutterie tried again, and again was driven back by great, curving teeth bared clear to the gums.

"Let Reese shoot it," Bensen said.

"I don't want to kill the dog," Gutterie said. "Looky the way she pulled her master up out of the water. There is something special about an animal what would do a thing like that."

LaVoie moved up alongside Gutterie. "If we are gonna do any good for that fellow, we need to get to him soon."

Gutterie frowned, perplexed, and glanced over his shoulder at Reese, shaking a charge of gunpowder into the priming pan. "We got any of that venison left, Reese?"

"A little."

"Toss me a piece of it."

"You're wasting time, Rudd. Let me shoot the dog and be done with it."

"Get me the meat, Reese," Gutterie snapped.

Reese frowned. "Sure, whatever you say, Rudd." He handed the rifle to Soute and went into the cabin. He returned with a chunk of cooked meat and threw it across the twenty feet of water. Gutterie sliced off a strip of it. "Here you go, girl." He moved a step forward cautiously. "Have some of this here venison, girl."

Her bark and her sudden advance drove Gutterie into deeper water. Bensen said, "Like I told you, Rudd, I've seen a dog guard a corpse for over a week. Couldn't even get near to him until hunger drove the animal off.''

"Well, that feller there ain't got a week to wait for that dog to get hungry." With a deep regret, Gutterie said, "All right, Reese, go ahead and shoot the dog."

Reese Sculty put the rifle to his shoulder and took aim.

Then the man on the shore moved. Gutterie was certain of it. He threw up his hand and said, "Wait a minute, Reese!"

Sculty lowered the rifle, perturbed at the delay.

The man said something too low and weak for Gutterie to hear, but his words instantly drew the dog to his side. His hand moved then, slowly, as if anchored down by a hundredweight of shot. His fingers folded lightly about the dog's leg.

Gutterie advanced a step and this time the dog remained seated. LaVoie and Bensen followed a few steps behind, and in another moment they were by the man's side. He was pale, and cold, and he'd lost a lot of blood. He groaned low and painfully from deep inside as they rolled him over. His gray eyes fluttered open and they looked Gutterie in the face.

"You sure enough are bad hurt, mister. What done it to you, Indians?"

The man's vision seemed drift out of focus. He struggled to speak, and then he lost consciousness.

McKendree came awake momentarily as they laid him on a flat surface. Overhead, threads of daylight came through wooden slats. He was aware of a gentle rocking motion, and for some peculiar reason he thought of his mother. All at once he smelled the odor of her cooking, a pleasant fragrance he'd not known for years. In a fever-induced delirium, he thought suddenly that he must be back in her kitchen—back in Tennessee. Then he was in her lap once again, curled up safe and warm, listening to the creak of the old rocking chair as it gently lolled him to sleep. . . .

A fierce pain in his side brought him suddenly awake. He wanted to scream out. His face was moist, and someone was wiping it with a rag. Overhead, a face he recalled having seen before peered at him. The gray whiskers seemed to bunch up around his mouth, and concern made itself known in the deep lines carved across his forehead.

"We took it out, mister," the whiskered face said. He held the long knife up for him to see.

McKendree nodded his head and tried to hold on to a consciousness that was slipping away like smoke through his fingers. "Where —where am I?" he said in less than a whisper.

"You're aboard my boat," the whiskered-faced man said. "My name is Rudd Gutterie. Don't you go worrying about it, mister. We'll take you someplace safe."

McKendree swallowed hard. It felt as if someone was building a fire beneath him. His vision blurred again and he struggled to keep the face in view. "The dog?" he asked, forcing the words out.

"She's right here," Gutterie said.

Someone took McKendree's hand and placed it upon a furry head. A wet tongue dragged itself across the back of his hand, and that was the last thing McKendree remembered.

"I think the fever is finally breaking," a voice said. In McKendree's half-conscious state, he imagined Noreen speaking.

Heavy footsteps sounded on a dirt floor, a rough hand pressed upon his forehead. "You're right, Emma." This time McKendree did recognize the voice. It brought to mind gray whiskers and a worried frown. "When he wakes, try to get more of that broth down him."

The footsteps receded. A door opened somewhere in the room. Gutterie's words reached him from farther away this time. "Carlotta, run down to the spring and fetch us another bucket of water." The door shut. Somewhere else in what sounded to McKendree like a small room, a chair creaked heavily.

McKendree struggled to bring himself to full consciousness. Daylight brightened the dark world behind his eyelids, and with a searing pain like a handful of sand thrown in his face, he parted his lids and blinked. Tears came instantly. He shut his eyes hard against the stabbing light, and tried again more slowly. In degrees, the world around him came into focus.

Across the room Gutterie sat at a table, peering at some papers in his hands. The woman he had called Emma sat across from him, sewing. Gutterie looked somehow different now, and then McKendree realized he had shaved. The cabin was a small, tidy place, with a window by the door, and another above the bed where he was lying. There was an open door to another room in the wall at the foot of the bed. From his position, he could see the corner of a bed back there where sunlight filtering in from an unseen window fell upon a crocheted bedspread.

"I'm going to be leaving in the morning, Emma," Gutterie said, folding the papers and looking across the table at her.

The needle in her fingers stopped its precise movements over the hooped piece of cloth and she said, "More business, Rudd?"

He nodded his head. "Need to go up to Independence to deliver a load."

"Alone?" she asked with a hint of concern.

"I'll be sharing it with Finn and Janck."

McKendree could only see Emma's back from his position on the bed, but he heard the frown in her voice. "I wish you hadn't taken up with those two, Rudd."

"We're partners," he said firmly. "Besides, I need their boats. The *Gutt's Bucket* is not a big vessel."

Emma set her sewing on the table and said, "That's another thing, Rudd—"

He threw up his hand. "I know, Emma. I know you think the name is vulgar. You've said it before and I don't care to hear it again."

"Well, it is. Such a handsome boat as it is, it deserves a proper name."

"I like the name," he said, rattling the papers in his hand impatiently, burying his nose back into them.

The door opened and a young girl stepped inside, the heavy bucket of water in her hand dragging down her left shoulder. She set it on a table by the window and when she turned she stopped suddenly and said, "Oh!"

McKendree gave her a smile.

"Papa, he's awake!"

Rudd Gutterie and Emma came about. "Well," Gutterie said, standing. "You finally come back from the dead, did you?"

"How long?" McKendree said, aware of the grating sound of his own voice. He swallowed and felt shoe leather in his mouth.

Emma's soft, cool hand cupped his forehead. "You've been unconscious for three days. Near delirious, I should say. But you'll be fine now. The fever is gone."

McKendree looked around and said, "The dog?"

"Carlotta, call the dog," Gutterie said.

The girl opened the door and clapped her hands. In a moment Duchess bounded through the open doorway and slid to a stop by McKendree's bedside, her tail thumping the floor and her tongue seeking his face. McKendree grinned and tried to fight her off, but he lacked the energy and even the slightest movement sent waves of pain up his side.

"Come on, girl," Gutterie said, using all his strength to haul the big dog off. "Let him mend some before you go givin' him all your love. Carlotta, put her out."

Carlotta took Duchess by the scruff of her neck and the dog immediately settled down and allowed the girl to take her outside.

"Fine animal you got there," Gutterie said. "She's good around kids."

"Her name is Duchess."

"And your name is?"

McKendree looked at him, then said, "It's Josiah. Josiah McKendree. From Miller County."

"You're a long ways from home, Mr. McKendree."

"Am I?" He didn't know where he was, only that he had to find Ribalt, and that meant he'd have to be moving on soon.

"You must be starving," Emma said. "I've only been able to feed you a little chicken broth."

Emma Gutterie was a plain woman but McKendree sensed that beneath the simple exterior resided a woman of deep convictions. Again he thought of Noreen, and he wanted desperately to know that she was all right—that she'd be standing in their cabin doorway when he returned. Life could never be the same without Lucas, he knew sadly, but at least with Noreen at his side they could weather the years ahead together, could work at rebuilding their lives.

Gutterie said, "You feel up to eating?"

McKendree heard the question distantly. He freed his brain from the thoughts that were piling one upon the other and said, "What?"

Gutterie grinned. "I asked if you was feeling up to some of Emma's chicken broth."

McKendree wanted to eat, even though the thought of it made his stomach turn somersaults. He had to regain his strength, and he needed food and rest to do so. He had to be strong when he set out once more for Ribalt. And then he could return home to Noreen. . . .

He stopped his thinking right there, not daring to consider any other alternative.

SEVENTEEN

IT WAS DARK when McKendree woke again. There was a candle burning on the table, and another in the back room where its feeble light danced upon the wall. He felt stronger, for the food that Emma Gutterie had fed him earlier had sat well with him, and he had gone to sleep tired but comfortable. Now, alone, he hitched himself up on his elbows, wincing at the sharp pain that shot along his side, and arranged the pillow so that he could sit up.

He moved aside the covers and discovered he was wearing a bed-shirt. Rudd Gutterie's, he reckoned, pulling a corner of it up high enough to examine the bandage wrapped about his waist. He touched it, experimentally, and felt the tender muscle beneath it. There was no blood on the bandage and McKendree figured it had been changed a time or two since his arrival.

He pulled the covers back on. The evening was cool, and the breeze coming through the open window carried with it the smell of the river. A shadow moved in the back room, riveting his attention. The sounds of someone moving around back there reached his ears.

"Hello," he said.

Carlotta's face appeared around the corner. Her eyes brightened and a smile puckered her cheeks. "You're awake again, Mr. McKendree," she said happily, coming into the room. "You slept much better this afternoon. Ma says you're on the mend. She says you are a very lucky man."

He smiled at the child. Carlotta Gutterie was a year or two

younger than Sarah Goodwin, he figured. "I'm a lucky man because your father found me and pulled me out of the river."

She shook her head. "Papa says you're built like a Kentucky mule, and that that's why you're still alive. He says a fall from those cliffs should have killed you right out. Ma says you got an angel riding on your shoulder."

They heard scratching at the door. Carlotta opened it, letting Duchess into the room. McKendree scratched the dog behind the ear and said, "This here is my angel." He frowned then, suddenly remembering George Winfield. He had attributed those same qualities to him too, and look how he ended up. McKendree was not a superstitious man, but all at once he wished he had not said those words.

"Papa says he'd never seen a dog as good as Duchess. He says she's a treasure."

"That she is," McKendree said, remembering how Duchess used to frolic with Lucas, or walk at Noreen's side when she went to gather raspberries on the hillside behind their cabin. McKendree had never worried about Noreen or Lucas when Duchess or Duke was along. If he had only made the dog stay at home that day. . . .

The sound of a door opening rescued him from the thoughts that were about to follow. Emma Gutterie wore a shawl around her shoulders, and a printed linen kerchief held her red hair back out of her face. "Feeling well enough to sit up, are we?" she said.

"I'm liable to start getting bed sores if I don't, Mrs. Gutterie."

She came over and laid a hand on his head. "No fever. Your color is lookin' better too. Hungry?"

McKendree was surprised, but he was hungry, even though he had not done anything but sleep. "I reckon I am," he said. "Where is Rudd?"

"He's out," she said, turning to the iron pot suspended in the hearth. Emma Gutterie stirred it with a long wooden spoon and said, "He had a meeting with some people. Something to do with his business. He doesn't talk much about his business." She ladled stew into a wooden bowl, then pulled a chair around and sat at his side. "Think you can handle this yourself or do you want help?"

"I can manage," he said, gingerly moving his arm and taking the food.

She smiled and said, "You sure about that?"

"I need to move or I'll stiffen up for sure."

"I'll get you a piece of bread." She went to a wooden cabinet. When she returned she sat back down and looked at him. McKendree stopped his slow progress with the spoon, uncomfortably aware of her gaze. He set the spoon down and found her eyes on his face.

"What happened to you, Mr. McKendree?"

He wasn't certain he was prepared to say anything about it . . . yet. To make it easy on himself, he said, "I ran across some ill-tempered men and we didn't see eye to eye."

"Indians?"

"There were a few of them there."

Her face grew concerned. "I feared that might be the case," she said. "They've mostly been peaceful the last few years. But I always worry about them—especially with Rudd away so often."

McKendree dipped a corner of the bread in the stew. "I wouldn't worry too much about it, Mrs. Gutterie. It was more a personal thing. I don't think there is any trouble brewing. Leastwise, I haven't heard of any." He bit the bread. Even his jaw muscles hurt to use them.

Emma Gutterie glanced at the bedroom where her daughter was. McKendree could see Carlotta's shadowy movements in the candle-light back there. Emma laughed nervously, as if releasing a troubling thought, and said, "You know, when you have children, you worry about things like that, especially in a half-tamed country like this. Why, we aren't but a hundred miles from wild territory, and the stories one hears coming out of the west are enough to make a decent man or woman turn gray. It wasn't so long ago that savages were carrying off women and children, and scalping husbands and fathers right here—in Missouri!"

McKendree wanted to tell her that savages were still doing that right here in Missouri, and that not all of them had red skin, either. But he saw no point in going into his own story, which is what would have surely followed if he had. He merely said, "Yes, ma'am," continuing the painful task of eating.

"Do you have any children, Mr. McKendree?"

He lowered his spoon and looked at her. She must have seen

something frightening in his eyes, for she immediately looked away from him and stood. "I, ah . . . I best get Carlotta to bed. It's . . . it's way past her bedtime." She hurried out of the room. Mc-Kendree watched after her a long moment. He didn't know what she had seen in his face just then. He wasn't even certain of his own feelings now—except that a bone-weary tiredness had overtaken him and was dragging down his eyelids again.

He set the half-eaten stew aside and moved his pillow back in place. Then he was asleep.

A sound pulled McKendree from a deep sleep. Although his body was injured, his senses remained razor keen. He opened his eyes to darkness, and the shape of a man standing in the doorway.

The man stepped into the cabin, a little unsteady on his underpin-nings, and immediately the room was awash with the smell of whis-key. McKendree figured the hour to be late night or early morning, and he wondered if Gutterie often came home from business meet-ings stone drunk and swaying like corn stalks in an October wind. Something else slipped into the room with him before the door closed with a bang. That something else positioned itself between McKendree and Gutterie, and her tail made a rapid sweeping sound against the floor.

"Shhhhh," Gutterie said with a finger pressed against his mouth. Duchess cocked her head at him.

"Rudd?" Emma's voice came from out of the darkness; a hushed but firm sound. "Rudd, get in here and be quiet!"

Gutterie staggered to the passageway, bumped something and cursed softly. McKendree lay in the dark listening to their low talk in the next room.

"You're drunk again," Emma declared. A candle flickered to life, and shadows danced upon the wall. "And you've been brawling again, Rudd," she said, disappointed, but with no reproach in her voice. "Let me look at that eye. It's gonna be swollen shut for sure in the morning. Rudd, why do you do this?"

"I had me a disagreement with Finn."

McKendree heard Emma's footsteps, saw her bedgown flash past him as she came into the room. In the darkness she dipped a cloth into a bucket of water, then returned to the back bedroom. "What did you two fight about this time?"

"Oww! Easy, Emma. Careful. It's not important."

"It was obviously important enough to get you a black eye!"

"I don't want to talk about it, Emma."

"You never want to talk about it."

"I'm tired."

"You're drunk."

McKendree heard a short laugh, and then the heavy creak of the bed as Gutterie sat down. "I want to go to sleep."

"Rudd, you're impossible sometimes."

"We'll talk about it in the morning, Emma," he said and his voice seemed to drift off. In a moment there came soft snoring. The candle flickered a few minutes longer before being snuffed out. Darkness engulfed the little cabin.

The next morning Rudd Gutterie seemed particularly unhappy as he felt his way from the back room to the kitchen table and sat slowly down. His left eye was black and swollen, and the right eye looked only a little better, with threads of red crisscrossing it. Gutterie held his head in his hands and asked for a cup of coffee. Emma set the coffee before him, said not a word and turned abruptly to McKendree.

"You feel up to coffee this morning, Mr. McKendree?"

The odor of it brewing had awakened him, and at the moment he could think of no better way to start the day. "Yes, ma'am."

She moved a stool near the bed and set a steaming cup upon it. Then she fixed breakfast. Neither she nor Rudd spoke during the meal, and when it was finished she said, "I believe Mr. McKendree's bandages should be changed, Rudd. Will you see to it while Carlotta and I are out?"

He nodded his head and grunted. She gathered the dishes into a tub, washed them, then tied a bonnet about her head and took Carlotta by the hand.

When they had gone, Rudd grinned sheepishly at McKendree and pushed himself up from the table. "She's mad at me."

"Oh?"

Rudd pulled a chair around and sat by his side. A frown contorted his round face where gray whiskers had begun to sprout again. "Yeah. I got back late, and I was drunk."

"It looks to me like you walked into a low tree branch, too."

He laughed and then grimaced, putting a hand to his head. "I looked when I should have ducked."

"I know the feeling."

"I'll just bet you do." Gutterie reached under the bed and came up holding McKendree's long knife. "Remember this?"

"It's my knife."

"What was it doing run clear through you then?"

McKendree grinned. "I looked when I should have ducked."

Gutterie chuckled and said, "You don't want to talk about it?"

"I'd rather not."

"Emma told me this morning you said something about it being Indians."

"That was only part of it. The trouble was of a personal nature. I told her that too. There was a white man there, and it's with him I have a score to settle."

"Hmmm." Gutterie thought a moment. "You in trouble with the law?"

"No."

"You usually attract trouble?"

"Not usually."

"Then it must be coincidence," he said cryptically.

"What do you mean?" McKendree saw the sudden look of concern that had come to Rudd Gutterie's face.

"Nothing . . . nothing at all." Gutterie flipped the knife over and handed it to him by its staghorn handle. "Only, maybe you best keep this someplace handy. Now, let's take a look at those bandages."

EIGHTEEN

RUDD GUTTERIE took the footpath down to the pier where the *Gutt's Bucket* was moored. The hour was near four o'clock, and when he stepped aboard Reese Sculty stuck his head out the cabin door. "We got word from Finn this morning. We're ready to shove off, Captain." Sculty whistled softly. "What happened to you?"

"I walked into a low branch," Gutterie said, remembering Mc-Kendree's comment. He handed Sculty a cargo manifest for a steamboat named *Morning Glory* and said, "She'll be moored at Hermann next week; heavy laden and bound for St. Jo."

Karl, LaVoie, Soute and Bensen filed out of the cabin to gawk at Rudd's shiner. He ignored their hoots and went aft to check the rudder pedestal, then he spent a moment studying the water with the practiced eye of a surgeon. "All right then, boys, let's shove off. We'll be meeting up with Finn and Janck at the cave. Sculty, think you can handle another side-wheeler?"

He grinned. "Same plan as with the *Laurel?*"

"The same game, Reese. It worked fine once, it should go again one more time before the river authorities catch on. All right, men," Gutterie said with the snap in his voice of one in command, "look sharp, we're shoving off."

They pushed out into the current and Rudd took the rudder. Standing atop the cabin's roof he had a clear view of the river ahead, and of the snags that appeared and disappeared as if with a mind of their own. The cave was less than a mile as the river flowed. There was a footpath from Gutterie's cabin, through the woods, to the cave. It was longer, and he seldom used it, preferring the flat, open water to the up and down of the narrow footpath. When the pier came into view off his starboard point, Gutterie steered a course toward it and the two other keelboats that rocked gently against the wooden pilings.

They tied up behind a keelboat named *Beaver Tail,* and clumped down the pier. The *Deborra,* Finn's boat, was moored on the upriver side of the pier. Some of Finn Johnson's crew were aboard her, and judging from the sounds coming from her cabin, Gutterie figured Johnson's men were well on their way to getting drunk. Benjamin Stye stuck his head out the doorway as they strode past. "Yo, Rudd," he said.

Gutterie stopped and looked back at him.

"Finn and Janck are waitin' for you at the cave."

Gutterie nodded his head. He and his men stepped off the pier. A few dozen steps from the river the mouth of the cave yawned before them.

"Afternoon, Rudd," a voice called down to him.

Up the side of the limestone cliff, Sam Katcham waved an arm at him. Katcham was one of Janck Hennigan's men. A rifle rested across Katcham's knees and a bottle of whiskey balanced precariously on a rock at his elbow.

"Afternoon, Sam."

LaVoie said, "Looks like they've all got a head start on us, Rudd."

"It might be best if we stayed sober tonight, boys."

Soute said, "You expectin' trouble, Rudd?"

Gutterie thought a moment. "I just don't want nothing to go wrong." He figured his disagreement with Finn Johnson the night before was none of their concern—at least, not yet it wasn't.

There was a doorway built into the cave a few feet from the entrance. Beyond it, the cave went back farther than anyone of Rudd's acquaintance had ever explored—but the first twenty rods of it was illuminated by torches along the walls. It opened up to a large room where Finn and Janck sat on chests, waiting. Their men were fitted in here and there—wherever they could find a place to sit among the crates, and bales, and barrels stacked in piles and lining the passageway. There was a cask of whiskey on its side. Walter

Helm was filling a long-neck bottle from it when Rudd and his men came in.

Janck stepped off a cask of gunpowder where he was smoking a cigar and stuck out a hand. "We've been waiting for you, Rudd," he said, offering him a bottle.

Gutterie clasped hands but shook his head at the whiskey. "Maybe later," he said. His words echoed off the slick walls and mingled with the low conversations going on around him. Gutterie's men drifted off to join the others while Rudd, Janck and Finn moved to one side.

Finn Johnson was a black-eyed French and Indian mix, with some Negro blood thrown in for good measure. He'd come up from Louisiana some years earlier and begun working the river as a lone wolf. When he joined up with Rudd and Janck, he decided his place ought to be top dog—he had been debating the issue with Rudd since. Finn looked at Rudd now and said, "That eye is lookin' right nasty, Rudd."

Gutterie grinned. "It smarts some. I'm pleased to see your nose has finally stopped bleeding."

Finn gently touched the purple and swollen protrusion. "I wanna thank you for this, Rudd. I studied it right careful in the mirror and I think you done went and busted it straight ag'in. Last time it was crooked as hell."

"Hey, you two, we got business to take care of," Janck said, putting himself between Rudd and Finn.

Gutterie sat beneath a sputtering torch on a ledge of rock and said, "I got hold of this manifest from a clerk in the office of the Masterson Steamboat Line. It's for a side-wheeler by the name of *Morning Glory.*" He grinned. "I told you last night I got something good. It's showing a cargo of flour, broadcloth, whiskey, beaver traps, rifles and one hundred and twenty-five barrels of gunpowder. There are some other trade goods, trinks mostly. The sort of things the savages out west like; mirrors, beads, knives, iron arrowheads. We might find a market for it if we care to run up the river beyond St. Jo."

"Lemme see it," Finn said.

Gutterie handed it over and Finn squinted in the feeble light at it. His mouth slowly took on the shape of a smile and he said, "Us can git good money fer the flour, and the gunpowder can be parceled out to the settlements without attracting attention. It looks like a promising venture."

Janck glanced at the manifest and handed it back to Rudd. "What did that cost us?"

Gutterie folded it into his pocket. "The clerk wants a hundred dollars. I told him he'd get it once the take is disposed of."

"A hundred dollars!" Finn said.

Gutterie eased him down with a wave of his hand. "Consider it an investment. He gets his hundred dollars, and we get more of these." He patted his pocket.

Janck pursed his lips and thought. "I think Gutterie is right. The flour alone will bring ten times that."

"It seems a hell o' a lot for to give to some clerk in a steamboat office, that's all."

"Not if he gets us more manifests," Gutterie said.

"So, what your plan?" Janck said.

Gutterie grinned. "I'll have me a sip of that whiskey, now, if you please."

Janck called for one of the men to bring a bottle. Gutterie wet his lips with it and sleeved the overflow off his chin. "My plan is this. Next week, Saturday, that's eleven days from today, I'll run the *Gutt's Bucket* down river to Hermann and we'll put in about a mile above the town. Reese and some of our men will board the *Morning Glory* while most of her crew is ashore. When they shove off, Reese and the others will get rid of the captain and his officers, and take over the pilot house. Reese was a pilot on the Mississippi a spell and he knows how them big boats operate."

Gutterie paused to study their faces. They seemed interested and he continued. "Meanwhile, you two take your boats upriver to the sandbars north of Sandy Hook and wait for us. Reese will run the *Morning Glory* aground there. If all goes smoothly, our men will dump the captain and his men overboard downriver, and by time the authorities get wind of it, we'll have the goods loaded and be long gone."

Janck thought the plan had merit, and reluctantly, Finn agreed.

"Good," Gutterie said, standing. "Then if that's settled, what say we get some of this stuff loaded up and see what we can peddle to those fine folks in Independence? Most of it should be cold enough by now not to attract too much attention."

Finn Johnson was a wiry man, and when he stood his eyes peered at the top of Gutterie's head. Just the same, Gutterie outweighed Finn a good thirty pounds and in a scrap they were a fair match. Finn Johnson shifted a cigar from one corner of his mouth to the other. "Us ain't done yet, Gutterie," he said, putting himself in Rudd's way.

"I figured we settled this last night, Finn," Gutterie said. He did not fear this man, but just the same, Finn Johnson was a formidable opponent.

Finn said, "Us got a smooth operation here, Rudd. Me'n some o' the boys been talkin', and us thinks bringing that man, McKendree, inside o' your house just m'be puttin' we all in peril. Him's an outsider, and him's too close to our operations. If him gits wind o' it, it mean pretty good the end o' a lucrative business, and m'be the end of a rope fer all o' we, too."

"Is that right, Rudd?" Andre LaVoie said from the side.

Gutterie glanced at him. "McKendree ain't gonna learn anything —hell, he can't even get out of bed."

"But him will be in time," Finn said. "What the hell make you pull him out of the river like you done?"

Gutterie had considered that very same question himself, and he had come up with no satisfying answer. It was a thing he'd done without thought. If he had, he'd most likely have passed McKendree by. After all, he'd put more than one body in the river himself. He grinned and said, "I reckon I was drunk at the time," and to emphasize the point, he took a long pull from the bottle in his hand.

The tension in Finn's face eased. "Then it will be a easy thing to fix, Rudd. Just"—Finn dragged a finger across his throat—"an' dump him body in the river."

"No."

The men gathered around. Gutterie was aware of them pressing close, curious. Even his own men showed more than mild concern on their faces.

Reese Sculty said, "You know, Rudd, I figured right from the beginning we ought to let McKendree be."

LaVoie and Bensen mumbled their agreement.

"McKendree is a guest in my house," Gutterie said, realizing the majority opinion was for a swift removal of the problem. "And while he is, he is under my protection." More than anything, it was a point of honor with Rudd Gutterie, and he had so little of that, he figured he ought to hold on to whatever there was.

Reese said, "If you don't want to do it, Rudd, I will. Finn is right. He could learn too much. Personally, I don't care to swing just yet."

There was a chorus of agreement and muffled laughter from the men gathered there. The tide of opinion was running against him. He said, "McKendree is my business. If and when he becomes a threat, I'll decide what to do about it." He turned and forced passage through the knot of men, stopping in the middle of the cavern and coming about. "In the meantime, we got a business to run here, and part of that business is hauling this stuff up to Independence and turning a dollar on it. If anyone has any disagreements, I'll talk personally to 'em." Rudd's hand came to rest on the pistol in his belt and his eyes narrowed down.

No one cared to take Gutterie up on his invitation. The men slowly parted and went about the job of moving the pirated goods from the cave to the waiting boats outside. Janck took charge of his men, putting the incident aside. Finn stood there a moment longer, looking at Gutterie, then spun about and barked orders to his men.

Gutterie dropped his hand from the pistol and took a long pull from the bottle. That was a narrow one. He wasn't sure he could pull it off again if the men decided to side with Finn. It occurred to him that the struggle for power between Finn and himself was becoming intolerable, and that perhaps it was time he did something about that—before Finn had a chance to do it to him.

As he turned to the job ahead, he thought of McKendree, lying helpless back at his cabin. He'd given McKendree the knife, and a warning, but those would do little good if these men decided to do away with him. Why not let them have him and be done with the problem?

Gutterie considered this avenue as he worked. He didn't understand the change that had come over him, but something inside refused to betray the man after he'd offered his friendship.

Gutterie frowned, tossed the bottle aside and went out to the *Gutt's Bucket* to supervise its loading.

NINETEEN

McKENDREE HEALED QUICKLY, and by the third day of his returning to consciousness he was on his feet puttering his slow and painful way around Rudd's cabin. It was Friday, and Rudd had been away three days. Emma had told him Rudd went up the river to Independence on business. When he had asked what sort of business, he drew a long silence from her, and then an elusive answer about hauling freight.

Well, it wasn't any of his concern, he thought as he sat at the table sipping coffee and turning the pages of a two-month-old copy of the *Missouri Republican*. He was thankful for their hospitality, and their help, but when he was well enough to travel, he'd put this part of his journey behind him and strike out after Jacques Ribalt. He knew exactly where he would find the man. Duchess lay at his side and raised her head as the door opened.

"Hello, Mr. McKendree," Carlotta said.

McKendree lowered the paper. Carlotta pulled back a chair and plopped a handful of dripping pebbles on the table.

"What you got there?"

"Indian jewels!" she said. "I found 'em in the river. Papa say an Indian princess lost 'em. She made a witch doctor mad at her and he turned all her pretty jewels into plain old rocks. It made the princess cry, and when her tears fell on the rocks they turned back into jewels. Now every time they get wet they turn back into jewels." She held a piece of quartz to the morning light coming through the window. "See," she said, handing it to him. "Don't it look pretty?"

"It sure does, Carlotta. I never heard that story about the princess." He dropped the pebble back into her hand.

Carlotta gathered them all up and deposited them securely in a leather pouch. "It's just something Papa made up when I was little. But it's fun to pretend, don't you think?"

He thought of Lucas pretending a tree branch was a rifle, or the tree stumps behind the corn field were crouching Indians in the evening dusk.

"Mr. McKendree? Are you all right?"

He looked at her and forced a smile to his lips. "Yeah. I'm just fine," he lied. "Where's your mother?"

"She went up the hill to visit with Mrs. LaVoie. She'll be back shortly."

That was the first McKendree had heard of neighbors. Being cooped up the way he was, he had no idea what the world in this bend of the river looked like. "Do you have many neighbors?" he asked her.

"No, not many. There is Andre and Martha LaVoie, up the hill a piece, and Bill and Wilma Bensen down the footpath about a mile. Then west of here a ways lives Reese Sculty. He ain't married, and none of the others have any kids either. They all work with my papa."

"You have any friends around here?"

Carlotta frowned and looked at the leather pouch in her hand, moist from the wet stones it held. "No, we're too far out to meet many folks. But I find things to do. When Papa's home he plays with me and tells me stories. Ma teaches me sewing and candle making, and I'm a real good cook, too."

"There are no towns nearby?"

"None near enough to walk to. We sometimes go down the river to Hermann in Papa's boat, or up to Jefferson City when Ma needs cloth and other store-bought things. But mostly Ma and me stay here and take care of things while Papa is away."

"He's away a lot?"

Carlotta nodded her head. "Sometimes for weeks. Then he comes home with lots of pretty things for Ma and me." Carlotta stopped to think. "It's funny, but those nice things don't make Ma happy. She keeps telling Papa he ought to find a different way to make a living. Then he gets drunk and hauls all those nice things down to the cave for 'safe keeping.' "

"What sort of things does your pa ship?" McKendree asked, remembering Emma's elusive answer.

Carlotta shrugged her shoulders. "Whatever he can, I reckon. He and his men, they make lots of plans and spend lots of time in the cave. That's all I know."

"Hmmmm." McKendree pushed himself up from the table. "How would you like to accompany an old invalid outside for a breath of air?"

"What's an *invalid*, Mr. McKendree?"

He grinned. "That's what I am."

She looked at him oddly, then said, "All right. I'll show you where I found the Indian jewels."

He started for the door, then remembered Gutterie's words of warning. He slipped the long knife into its scabbard on his belt. A series of small steps brought him outside. The wide river lay a half-dozen rods from the front door. He scanned the curve of it—what he could see from his vantage point—then eased himself along a steep footpath to the pier where a skiff was tied. The morning was warm, and the air heavy with the odor of rushes and moist earth. It was a pleasant place, but the broad waterway and the open sky made McKendree vaguely uneasy for a reason he did not understand. He attributed it to his present state of mind and body, and the knowledge that the longer he stayed in this place the longer it would be before Ribalt accounted for all the wrong he had done.

"Feel up to walking onto the pier?" Carlotta asked.

McKendree looked down at her. "Give me a shoulder to lean on?"

She smiled up at him, stretched an arm around his waist and together they walked out onto the slender anchorage of timbers and pilings that reached out into the water.

McKendree spent most of the next day in a chair by the water's edge, listening to the life-sounds of a living river, growing more at ease with it as he shaved a length of wood into a pile of curled slivers, ending up with a crutch. He cleaned his pipe, dried the tobacco he carried in a pouch in his hunting bag and smoked a half-dozen bowls as he felt his strength slowly return. When he tired of sitting, he experimented with the crutch and strolled a short distance along the river. He explored another trace that cut back into the forest—stopping at a point where it inclined toward the ridge line.

Emma Gutterie fed him a noon meal and he helped Carlotta retrieve more Indian jewels from the river. Rudd Gutterie returned later that afternoon, tied the keelboat at the pier, and his men departed for their various homes. McKendree felt their coolness toward him as he stood there, watching them dock and leave, but Gutterie greeted him with a firm handshake and dropped a pouch into his hand.

"What's this?" McKendree asked, smelling the tobacco in the chamois pouch.

"European . . . I think. See, that ain't no American writing. I happened across it in Independence and figured you'd find it pleasing." He gave McKendree a wry smile. "I went through your hunting bag before you regained consciousness—just to try and learn who you were, you understand," he added quickly.

McKendree tried to pronounce the word branded on the leather pouch, and stumbled over his tongue.

Gutterie laughed. "Andre says it's German. I couldn't say for sure, but it do look like the same funny writing on a cardboard Nativity that Emma sets up each Christmas, and I know it's from Germany."

They returned to the cabin, where Gutterie passed out gifts. McKendree fished a brand from the fireplace and put it to a bowl of the German tobacco. He sat back to watch Emma adjust a bright red shawl over her shoulders and look at herself in a mirror. Carlotta learned to operate a wooden doll on a stick that lifted its legs and arms at the tug of a string. Gutterie seemed thoroughly pleased with himself, but after a few moments, Emma replaced the shawl in its cardboard box, and with a sudden look of sadness, hurried into the back room.

Gutterie frowned. He quickly changed to a smile when he noticed McKendree studying him. "Women," he said. "Who can understand 'em?"

Rudd Gutterie remained home the next day. McKendree spent

the morning on the dock with him as he fussed around the boat and swept her deck clean. Gutterie seemed friendly enough, but McKendree sensed something deeper in the man; something he was trying desperately to keep hidden. That afternoon two of Rudd's men came down the footpath. McKendree became aware of them as they emerged from the forest on a trace he'd traveled upon a short distance the day before. He recalled their faces from the tortured glimpses he had had of them while drifting in and out of consciousness. He didn't know their names until Gutterie stuck his head out of the cabin door and said, "Reese, Andre." Gutterie wiped his hands on a dirty rag and stepped down to the pier. "To what do I owe this visit?"

They were stern-faced. They looked at McKendree with narrow eyes. Gutterie noticed it too. McKendree made note of their names. The one Gutterie had called Reese said, "We need to talk, Rudd."

"I'm listening."

"Alone." Reese glanced at McKendree.

McKendree said, "I'll let you three alone." He strolled off the pier, using the crutch less today than he had the day before. His side ached, but not unbearably so. As he started up the hill, he looked over his shoulder to find the three of them staring at him. He turned back to the cabin and discovered Emma standing in the doorway, peering past him at the men on the pier. There was a tightness about her lips, and her fingers clutched and released where they interlocked in front of her apron. She turned stiffly and disappeared into the cabin.

When McKendree arrived at the house, Emma was peeling potatoes as if the Lord had given her five minutes to skin a bushel of them before he would take her away. He stopped in the doorway and said, "Are you all right, Mrs. Gutterie?"

His words startled her. She dropped a potato and fumbled to recover it. "Why, of course, Mr. McKendree. What could be wrong?"

Her smile was a poorer liar than she was, he thought. He said, "You just looked concerned when Sculty and LaVoie showed up."

She laughed unconvincingly and turned back to the potatoes, moving at a more leisurely pace. "Oh, that's ridiculous. What could I possibly be concerned about? Reese and Andre are Rudd's friends.

They work for him. . . ." The knife in her hand paused. She turned back as if to say something further, then stopped, shook her head and said, "That's ridiculous."

Later, Rudd came in and said, "I have to leave for a while. I'll be back by supper."

Emma said only, "Be careful."

Gutterie looked at McKendree, started to speak, then looked away and left. McKendree stepped to the door in time to see the three men strike out on the trace that led into the forest.

McKendree came about to discover Emma staring out the window. There was trouble growing, like a warble beneath the skin; unseen, but easily felt. He felt it, and he sensed something else too —something he was determined to know the meaning of. If Emma wouldn't tell him, he'd learn it on his own.

TWENTY

McKENDREE SPENT the afternoon in Emma Gutterie's company, but feeling very much alone. She was distant. She spoke only when spoken to; politely, but with an economy of words that told McKendree her thoughts were clearly elsewhere. He asked her for a whetstone and she found one for him in a shed behind the house where Rudd kept his tools. A shovel and some files were there too, along with wood rasps, and block and tackle. He found a tin of oil and set about drawing a sharp edge on his knife. McKendree did not want trouble, but if it came, he'd be ready for it. He had no idea what had upset Emma so, or the reason for the icy reception Rudd's men had given him, but the learning of that was only a matter of time, he was certain.

As evening came, McKendree walked along the path Rudd, Reese and LaVoie had taken. When it inclined steeply toward the ridge line he had to stop. His side tightened up like a fist, and it ached like a burning lump of coal buried beneath his skin. It was still too soon for such exertion, and he returned to the cabin.

Carlotta was in the back room when he came in, softly singing a tune. Emma had dinner cooked and the table set. McKendree glanced around the room, searching for something he'd missed seeing since his arrival.

"You've been off for another walk, Mr. McKendree?" Emma asked. She seemed to have regained much of her poise, and if she was still worried, she didn't show it to him now.

"I did a bit of exploring, but I'm afraid I'm not up to much of that sort of thing yet. You live in a pretty little valley, Mrs. Gutterie, but it's all up and down walking. In a few more days, maybe. What with your good cooking and care, I'll be fit in no time."

"I'm glad. You'll be moving on then?"

McKendree detected an eagerness in her words he was certain she had not meant for him to hear. "I've got things to do," he said, thinking suddenly of Ribalt.

"You have a home in Miller County, you said. I'm certain you're anxious to get back to it."

"When I'm done with what I need to do."

Emma Gutterie studied him a moment, then said, "Is Noreen your wife's name?" That came unexpectedly. He looked at her with surprise. She said, "You spoke of her almost continuously while you were unconscious."

McKendree averted his eyes to his powerful hands. Large and rough hands they were, yet how easily they had fit into Noreen's. Instantly he longed for the touch of her hand against his. The concern he had borne for her, and had kept submerged all these many days, swept over him in an instant, like a river at flood level. He forcibly closed the floodgates of his mind and said, "Noreen is my wife."

Emma Gutterie sat across the table from him. "What happened, Mr. McKendree? What has been tormenting you so?"

He might have easily asked her the same question. But he didn't. A frown dragged down the corners of his mouth. McKendree was not a man to burden others with his problems, yet suddenly the hurt that he'd been carrying around with him since Ribalt had swept down onto his homestead and forever changed his life was too much to bear alone. Without realizing it, he was telling Emma Gutterie all . . . and when it was out, he felt strangely at ease with himself, as he had after telling Winfield. The hurt was still there, and his mission had remained unchanged, but now he seemed better able to stand back and see his course of action clearly, as if a brain fog had lifted, and bright light now picked out his next step in clear detail.

Emma poured him a cup of coffee. "You'll be finding this Jacques Ribalt then, when you leave here?" she asked, sitting back behind the table with a cup warming her hands.

"Yes, ma'am," he said. "Then I'll go home—" he paused to consider his next words—"and see what is left there for me."

"The Goodwins seem like fine friends." Now it was Emma's turn to pause and consider. "They'll be there, if nothing else." She saw the lines deepen in his face and added quickly, "I'll pray for you, and your wife." That didn't seem to help much.

"Thanks," he said, standing, leaving the coffee untouched.

"Where are you going?"

McKendree stopped at the door. "I'm going to walk down to the water."

"It can be peaceful on the river, especially on a clear night. Watch your step; it's easy to slip on that footpath in the dark."

McKendree tugged his hat onto his head and stepped outside. Moonlight glistened off the dark Missouri where the keelboat was moored. The sound of water moving through the pilings, the call of frogs and toads, the screech of crickets from under the cabin, all blended into a serenade that eased his strained nerves. McKendree started down the footpath but the sound of muffled voices reached him, destroying the moment. He moved quickly into the deeper shadows alongside the house as three shapes emerged from the forest.

"I don't know, Rudd," the voice McKendree recognized as belonging to Andre LaVoie said, "I think you're digging yourself into a hole this time. And being stubborn ain't gonna help matters any."

Reese Sculty said, "There is no point in being pigheaded. The boys have all said their piece. If you buck the wind, it's only going to capsize you."

Rudd Gutterie came to an abrupt halt. His two companions stopped too. He said, "What I'm hearing is that my own men are standing with Finn and Janck—standing against me."

There was a long pause. LaVoie said, "Not a man among us wants to go against you, Rudd, but there is more here to consider. For some reason you have gone and got a streak of Samaritan in you. I ain't sayin' that's all bad, but you got to think about what you're risking."

"You mean if he should learn what I really do on the river?"

"You know that's what we mean, Rudd," Sculty said impatiently.

"Finn and Janck made it plain enough. You either do something about it, or we'll do it for you."

Gutterie laughed softly. "It seems I might have me a mutiny on my hands."

"Mutiny? This ain't the high seas," LaVoie said, "but if you do have a mutiny, it will be of your own making. You can stop it right here—tonight. Everything will be like it used to."

"Hmmm," Rudd said.

"Well, what will it be?" Sculty asked.

"I ain't gonna do anything tonight . . . except think on it."

"You do that," Sculty said. "None of us want to go against you, but what Finn said makes sense. We got a good life here, and we are all wanted by the law. As long as they don't know who or where we are, we're safe. If that leaks out, we might as well put our affairs in order, for it'll be the end of a rope for us for sure. And Rudd, if it comes down to my neck, or his—or yours for that matter—well, the choice is clear to me."

LaVoie grunted his approval.

McKendree watched them part company. LaVoie and Sculty struck out in another direction while Gutterie stood in the dark watching them fade into the night. Gutterie seemed to sigh, and then with a heaviness to his step, he continued on to the cabin, passing within feet of where McKendree stood. With hardly a thought, McKendree's hand moved for the hilt of the knife on his belt. He stopped the movement. Gutterie passed, unaware, and McKendree eased back farther into the shadows, knowing safety lay in the darkness of the forest where human eyes could not see him.

In another part of the forest, many miles distant, Jacques Ribalt and Jimmy sat around a campfire. Ribalt knew his son was clearly unhappy, and he knew the reason why. Ribalt rose to his feet like an old, tired bear, and in the darkness, the fire lit the fringes of his beard.

"All right, you can stop brooding about it," he said. "I told you I'd get you that English gal, and I will. Soon as we get home. Only, there's gonna have to be a plan." He shook his head and peered down at the boy. "She ain't gonna come of her free will, and I can tell you right off, her pa ain't gonna give her to you." He looked around the dark encampment where fires burned and their light flickered off the scattered tepees, and said, "Since you got it in your head to have a woman, it'd be a whole lot easier on all of us if you'd pick one of the women here. They're more our kind of people."

"Pa," Jimmy said with growing impatience, "I want Sarah Goodwin, I don't want no Indian woman."

"Your ma's Indian. She was good enough to bear you."

"It ain't that there's anything wrong with 'em, Pa," Jimmy said. "But none of 'em have—well." He was suddenly embarrassed. "None of 'em have such yellow hair as Sarah. Or them sky-blue eyes like she has. And she smells—well, different."

"Different, how?" Ribalt asked, narrowing an eye.

Jimmy shrugged his shoulders. "I don't know. Just different. She smells . . . of soap. And her clothes, they smell fresh washed all the time."

"How many times have you smelled her clothes, boy?"

Jimmy looked back at the fire. "Only once, I reckon. But I remember it right clear."

Ribalt made a sound of disgust in his throat. "You'll come to your senses soon enough, once you marry the gal. All right, if the pickin's here ain't to your likin', we'll be off to home in the morning."

Jimmy poked at the fire with a stick. Ribalt hunkered down beside him and said, "You know we're gonna have to take that gal against her will."

"I know," he said, staring into the fire.

"You reckon you can tame a gal like that? One what's taken again' her likin'?"

Jimmy grinned. "I reckon I can. You said yourself that we can bring her round to our way of thinkin'."

Ribalt nodded his head. "We can, but it ain't gonna be easy. It's you, boy, what will have to put up with her."

"I can handle her, Pa. I'll handle her like you handled Ma."

Ribalt laughed and grabbed a handful of his son's coarse black hair, pulling his head back. "I see a lot of me in you, boy. I like that."

Jimmy smoothed his hair down. "I had me a good teacher, Pa."

Ribalt stood. "I reckon I'll go find your grandpa. See if between us, we can't come up with a plan, and some braves to help us out with it."

"I'm comin' with you." Jimmy was up on his feet and the two of them strode off into the night.

TWENTY-ONE

MCKENDREE KEPT SILENTLY behind Sculty and LaVoie, yet near enough to hear their low conversation. He moved with the stealth of a panther, and while he threaded his way through the trees, he sketched out the bare beginnings of a plan. He needed to learn more of what they had in mind for Gutterie, and he wanted to fix in his brain the locations of their cabins. Beyond that, McKendree wanted time alone to think, to formulate his next move.

After a short distance, McKendree felt the first pangs of a tightening muscle in his side. He ignored them, not daring to allow the wound to force him to lose his quarry.

Sculty and LaVoie stopped then. McKendree drew up, melted into the shadows at the edge of the path and felt the ache in his side slowly ease.

Sculty said, "Andre, what do you think?"

LaVoie tilted his head up at the star-filled sky and slowly shook it. "I think Rudd's got a bee in his bonnet that ain't gonna be easily shaken."

Sculty grunted his agreement. "I knew it was a mistake to fish that stranger out of the river. I had a gut feeling no good could come out of it." He drew in a breath and snorted it out. "It's gonna be us who has to take care of him."

"That ain't gonna be easy, not with Rudd looking over him."

Sculty glanced at LaVoie, and in the darkness McKendree saw his angular face take on a frown. "Then I reckon we'll have to deal with Rudd too."

LaVoie didn't speak at once. When he did, he said, "I don't know, Reese. Rudd's been good for us."

"He's getting soft," Sculty shot back. "I'm not sure what it is about him, but something's changed. Five years ago he'd have thought nothing of leaving a stranger in the river. Now he's pulling 'em out and nurse-maiding 'em back to health. I don't like it. He did it once, he'll do it again. And one of these times it'll come back at us. Someone will figure out what we're up to here and that'll be the end of it."

"Maybe you're right, Reese," LaVoie said, unhappily.

"You know I'm right. Finn and Janck, they know what needs to be done. I say we cut both their throats and be done with it."

LaVoie stuck his hands into his pockets, clearly displeased with this solution to their dilemma. He said, "Let me think on it awhile, Reese."

"Sure, we got time. That stranger's not fit to travel yet, and there is still the job next week. We need Rudd and we need his boat for that. Afterward, when the stuff is safely stored in the cave, then we'll take care of both of them."

"What about Emma, and the girl?"

"What about 'em? You got Wilma to worry about, and your own neck. If we leave them around, they'll run to the authorities." Reese shook his head. "We get rid of Rudd, and we get rid of his family too."

LaVoie's head dropped to his chest. It shook once and he said, "We'll have to talk more about this later. Maybe Rudd will come round to his senses and take care of the problem himself."

"Even if he does, can we trust him not to do it again? I think not. It seems to me the time has come for us to part company with Rudd Gutterie . . . permanently."

McKendree listened to this, thinking of the people who had helped him in his time of need. In doing so they had put their own lives in peril. He wasn't yet strong enough to help Rudd if it came down to fists and knives. He no longer had a rifle, and he could not remember seeing one in Rudd's cabin. He recalled the pistol Rudd sometimes carried in his belt, but that wouldn't add much of an advantage once push came to shove.

LaVoie and Reese parted down separate paths. McKendree figured of the two, Reese was the most dangerous, and struck out after him. The footpath began to climb. The dull ache in McKendree's side swelled until he had to hold back. He lost ground as Reese strode ahead. By the time McKendree reached Reese's cabin, the door was shut and candlelight flickered behind a dingy window.

McKendree moved up to the wavy glass. Inside the one-room cabin were a single table and two chairs. Against one wall stood a bed with a rumpled blanket half fallen onto the dirt floor. The fireplace was cold, and the only food Sculty appeared to own was a side of venison hanging from the dark rafters. The cupboards stood open, and were empty. In the corner, McKendree could see a rifle leaning in the shadows.

Reese Sculty was seated at the table with an opened bottle of whiskey in his fist, peering at the window where McKendree knelt. Whatever Reese was seeing, McKendree figured it was something going on behind his eyes, not in front of them. After a few minutes, Reese set the bottle back onto the table and dropped onto the bed, half pulling the covers over him. It wasn't but another minute before he was snoring.

McKendree glanced at the corner where Reese's rifle stood. The candle flickered and guttered, struggling to keep alive—and it seemed to be losing. He turned away to give the situation some thought. If he were to leave tonight, Rudd and his family would be no better off than they were now. Reese wanted him out of the way, and although LaVoie seemed unwilling to go along with him at the moment, in the end, McKendree knew, he'd bend his way. Staying, he'd be in a position to give Rudd a hand when the time came—if nothing else, only to sound a warning, even as Rudd had given him a warning. Rudd must have known days ago that the tide of sentiment was turning against him. The decision was clear, and having made it, he turned back to the window.

In the failing light the rifle's long brown barrel shone invitingly. McKendree could think of several good reasons to take it, not the least of them being to deprive Sculty of its use. It might be a small thing, but any effort to tip the balance in his favor was a worthwhile endeavor. Reese snored away on the bed. A booted foot protruded from beneath the covers and vibrated with each breath, as if a thread connected the boot to his nose.

The candle flame struggled, flaring and then receding to something barely more than an ember. McKendree eased the door open. A gust of fall night air snuffed the flame, instantly throwing the cabin into deep blackness. McKendree breathed a bit easier and slipped into the cabin. His senses were alive. His ears measured the rhythm of Sculty's breathing, his feet seemed to see on their own the clutter scattered about. He felt a sudden surge of vitality he had not known for over a dozen years—a memory, safely hidden away, stole back into his brain. The dark cabin around him wavered and took on the shape of a smoke-permeated lodge. The sleeping man an arm's length away became the Shawnee warrior that had scalped his father and murdered his mother and sisters. Suddenly he was eighteen years old again. . . .

Without realizing it, he had moved toward Sculty and his long knife had cleared its sheath. His hand lifted and for a moment hung motionless in the air over the sleeping man. The apparition dissolved, and McKendree discovered his breathing was coming in pants. His face and hands were sweating. A glance told him the lodge had been a vision, built up from a fearful and long-forgotten memory. The heavy odor of whiskey in the air reminded him that the sleeping man beneath the point of his knife was white, not red.

McKendree lowered the knife, returning it silently to its sheath. He eased back and quietly lifted the rifle. In the darkness his fingers wrapped about a leather bag. Judging from its weight, it contained powder and shot. He took it too and started for the door. Then his heel came down on a tin can that crunched beneath his weight. Instantly, McKendree froze. Sculty snorted and turned upon the bed, but he slept on. Redoubling his caution, McKendree backed out of the cabin, closed the door to the chilling night air and retraced his steps.

In a tree some distance from Gutterie's cabin, he stashed the rifle and ammunition, and then he went inside. McKendree hadn't expected anyone to be up—and he was wrong.

Gutterie was seated at the table wearing a scowl and holding his pistol. The gun snapped up with authority as McKendree stepped inside, and its barrel steadied on his chest.

TWENTY-TWO

THE NEXT FEW SECONDS passed like a dozen slow minutes. McKendree noted the half-full bottle of whiskey at Rudd Gutterie's elbow. The look in Gutterie's eyes that he'd first thought was brooding, upon closer scrutiny, proved to be a liquor-induced stupor. The back room where Emma and Carlotta slept was dark. It was only Rudd Gutterie, and his gun, here to greet him. By McKendree's bed, Duchess lifted her head from off folded paws. Her tail sweeping back and forth told him that she, at least, was happy to see him. McKendree felt the thumping of his heart as an uncertain look flashed momentarily in Gutterie's eyes.

"McKendree!" The pistol barrel pointed to the ceiling, and Gutterie eased the hammer down. "Gracious, man, I nearly blowed your head off!" He set the pistol on the table, his hand shaking. "Where have you been? I figured for sure they—er, I mean you got yourself lost . . . or worse." His speech labored under the weight of too much drink. He was sweating heavily and he patted the sleeve of his shirt upon his forehead.

McKendree's reflexes eased off their hair-trigger set. He saw the fear in Gutterie's face. Was it for him? Or did Gutterie somehow know what Sculty and the others were planning?

"I went out for a walk," McKendree said, closing the door behind him. "Are you all right, Rudd?"

"No, I'm not all right. I've been a sittin' here the last hour figurin' you went and got yourself in trouble." He snatched the bottle off the table and took a drink, then offered it to McKendree.

McKendree shook his head. "No, thanks."

"I didn't figure you fit enough to go wandering around. You know, it ain't safe here. The river bank is mighty slippery in places, and the water can pull you down like a sea devil, it can."

"Are Emma and Carlotta asleep?"

"Huh? Oh, yeah, they went to bed a while ago."

McKendree sat across the table from Gutterie and said, "I appreciate you worrying about me, but I was in no trouble."

Gutterie drank more whiskey and said, "Well, until you're full-healed, you might best consider staying near. If not for your peace of mind, at least for mine. All kinds of peril lurks in them woods, 'specially once the sun goes down."

McKendree grinned. He'd grown up in the woods. He knew them as he had known the feel of his rifle's trigger the instant before the hammer fell . . . or the touch of Noreen's breath upon his neck as they slept. He said, "I appreciate the concern. Actually, I'm feeling quite fit." That wasn't the bald-face truth, but he figured it was the simplest explanation he could offer for being out and about only a week after stepping in front of the point of his own knife. "It seems that game is right plentiful in this area. I thought I'd do some hunting next week. Get some venison or bear meat to fatten your larder. It's the least I can do to pay you back for your hospitality. I have no money."

"I don't want your money, McKendree," Gutterie said.

"If you've got a rifle I can borrow, I'll bring you some meat."

"That ain't necessary, either."

"It's something I'd like to do, Rudd. Hunting is a thing I'm a fair hand at."

Gutterie rubbed his chin whiskers and thought a moment. He said, "If a man feels he owes a debt, then I reckon he ought to pay it. You don't, you understand, owe a debt that is, but if you really want to hunt us up some extra meat, well, I reckon Emma and Carlotta would appreciate it. Mostly, we eat catfish, and that's fine eating for sure, 'specially rolled in corn meal the way Emma fries 'em. But I'm rather partial to bear meat myself."

"Then bear it will be," McKendree said.

Gutterie frowned. "Only thing is, I ain't got a rifle. Ain't got no gun at all 'cept this here pistol."

"Mmmm." McKendree had another of his questions answered.

Gutterie's whiskey-sodden eyes brightened just a bit then. "But I do got a blunderbuss."

"A what?"

"Blunderbuss. It's older than I am. It once belonged to a British naval captain. I come by it some years ago through a . . . a business transaction," he said.

"I've heard of them, but I can't say as I ever seen one."

Gutterie stood, unsteadily. "I'll be right back." He went outside and McKendree heard him rummaging around in the dark behind the cabin. When he returned he carried a rolled deerhide under his arm. McKendree moved the whiskey bottle from the table and Rudd unfolded the hide.

"I ain't had this thing out since I got it," he said, lifting the short weapon and eyeing it, having trouble bringing it into focus. "Here, what do you think? Will it kill a bear?"

McKendree took the blunderbuss and moved the lamp nearer, turning up the wick. It was a short thing, ridiculously short, he thought at first, thinking of his own long, slim, tapered rifle that he'd lost in the woods during his fight on the palisades. This firearm wasn't any longer than his arm, and the flared muzzle gave it the appearance of being even shorter yet.

But closer examination showed the piece to have been finely crafted. The lock was engraved all over, except for a rectangular area where it had been stamped: J. Hawkins, London, 1765. The barrel couldn't have been any longer than sixteen inches, McKendree figured, rubbing a thumb over the Damascus steel and seeing the swirling layers of iron that had been hammer-forged together into shades of browns and yellows and blacks. He looked down the flared muzzle and reckoned that with not much effort, he could almost squeeze his hand down to the breech plug.

"Well?" Gutterie asked.

"It's a handsome thing, in its own peculiar way."

"I was told ship captains preferred them 'cause they was easy to load on a rolling deck. And 'cause you didn't have to aim to hit what you was shooting at."

The brass trigger guard caught and threw back some of the lamplight. McKendree figured with work it would shine like the day it left the gunsmith's shop. The bore was such that he could dump the contents of a full bullet pouch down it and still have plenty of room for powder and wadding.

"Figure you can bring down a bear with that, McKendree?"

He couldn't help but grin. "Probably bring down a whole bevy of bear if'n they're standing close together."

Gutterie laughed and reached for the bottle. "Then it's yours."

"Mine?"

"I ain't got no use for it, and you're sort of shy a gun at the moment. Never know when a man's gonna need a gun, 'specially in these parts. Now, you got grit enough to drink with me, or am I gonna have to get drunk all by myself?"

"You're already drunk, Gutterie."

"I'm only startin'." He offered the bottle again.

McKendree took it and studied the label pasted to it. "This is civilized booze." He tasted it, then swigged down a mouthful and handed the bottle back to Gutterie. "It ain't got much of a bite, Rudd, not like the stuff we brew back in Miller County."

Gutterie looked at him suspiciously. "And I thought you was just afraid of it, McKendree." He tasted the whiskey again, just to make sure, and made a face. "I'm not sure I'm grow'd up enough to try the stuff you brew in Miller County—not if this here John Barleycorn goes down your throat like honey."

"You'll have to come up sometime and try it," he said, taking the bottle back.

"I just might do that, when I'm in a daring mood."

They finished the bottle and Rudd staggered outside to find a second bottle aboard his boat. McKendree sat on the edge of his bed, scratching Duchess behind the ears. When Gutterie didn't return, he went outside to look for him. He found him down on the *Gutt's Bucket,* sound asleep. McKendree covered him with a blanket and went back up to the house to his own bed, but sleep didn't come at once.

He lay there, exhausted, with his thoughts, and his plans, and his memories keeping him awake until the window glass brightened with the dawn. Only then did he finally drift off to sleep.

The next day, McKendree gathered rags and files and oil, and spent the morning cleaning up the old blunderbuss, picking rust from the lock and fire-hole, polishing the brass furniture. And while he worked, he studied the problem that threatened him and the Gutteries. Up until now, he had only himself to worry about. Now there were three other people.

And there was still Ribalt. The fire of revenge had not gone out. McKendree ached for the moment he could close his fingers about the man's great, hairy throat. But he had time yet. Ribalt would not be going anywhere, and with him believing McKendree was dead, he'd not be looking for his return.

McKendree's thoughts finally came around again—as they did with the regularity of the passage of the hands upon the face of a clock—to Lucas. He grieved, and he worried after Noreen. And had Josiah McKendree known at that moment what Ribalt was planning, he would have dropped everything and left at once—despite his condition. But he didn't. In his mind, he still had plenty of time.

TWENTY-THREE

THURSDAY MORNING Sarah Goodwin felt painfully alone. Her brother Tommy was right there beside her, building a stick tepee on the ground, and her father was feeding the cow in the barn not a hundred feet behind the house, but still she knew what had to be the deepest emptiness of her young life. She wanted to cry, but not here, not where Tommy could see. . . .

"Sarah?"

Sarah turned her head, saw her mother standing on the porch. There was sadness in the angle of Rachael's mouth, and the lines of her face seemed pulled down. Her fingers clung to the wooden railing as if she could find security there. But Rachael knew that in this land there was no security; not behind thick log walls, not behind shuttered windows. They had not helped Noreen or Lucas. And now even Josiah was gone. His riderless horse returning in a lather had told them that.

Rachael drew in an unhappy breath. She admired her husband's devotion to his friend; his hopeful words, spoken less often now as McKendree's absence was going into its third week. Still, Charles walked down to the cabin twice a day, tended the livestock, and had made arrangements with other wide-flung neighbors to harvest his crops. Fall was already bringing a nip to the air and coloring the trees.

"Are you all right, dear?" she asked.

"Yes, Mama," Sarah said. That wasn't, of course, the truth. She was not all right. She missed Lucas McKendree dreadfully. Her young mind had found it almost impossible to admit he was gone—

forever. He had been younger than she, and now he was dead. It made her feel horribly vulnerable—and so very alone. They'd known each other all their lives, and now the emptiness of death left a hole in her world.

"Would you like to help me with the bread, honey?"

Sarah shook her head. "I don't feel like it, Mama."

Rachael felt Sarah's grief. She knew that each person had to work through it his own way. "Maybe your pa could use some help in the barn." Rachael also knew sitting around, moping, only made matters worse.

Sarah shrugged her shoulders and stood. "I reckon I'll just take a walk down to the creek for a while, to watch for turtles. I won't go far, Mama."

"Stay near enough to hear when I call you."

"I will." Sarah started toward the creek, head hanging and shoulders stooped. This dark mood would blow over in a few days, or a few weeks. Sarah was a resilient child, and grief had a way of working through a body in stages. She'd come through it, all right. Yet, seeing her child so affected made Rachael's own grief that much more difficult to cope with. Rachael watched Sarah make her way to the stream that flowed beyond the corn field and find a deadfall to sit upon at the water's edge. With a sigh, Rachael went back inside the house and to the bread that needed baking.

At the water's edge, Sarah allowed her pent-up tears to roll freely down her cheeks. She gathered a handful of pebbles from the muddy earth; dirty, unattractive things, unlike the shimmering pieces of quartz Carlotta Gutterie had called "Indian jewels." They might have been pretty had Sarah washed them in the flowing water, but she had never heard the story of the Indian princess. She barely looked at them now as she tossed them into the stream one at a time.

She was thinking of Lucas, and so consuming were her thoughts that she did not hear the footsteps come up behind her. Not that she would have heard them even if she had been listening. The three men approached with the stealth of a cat while back among the trees, two more men watched.

Then all at once a hand swept down over Sarah's mouth. She tried to cry out, but her scream remained trapped in her throat.

Strong arms lifted her off the ground. Sarah kicked. Another pair of arms folded about her legs, and when she tried to scratch, her captors pinned down her hands. It was only then that she caught a glimpse of their faces.

Sarah had grown up on the frightful stories of days not so long ago when the Shawnee would attack settlements, murder the men and carry off the women and children. Her father had told her those days were past, but she had never been quite convinced of that.

Now, staring at a face painted in war colors not six inches from her own, feeling hot breath upon her cheek, smelling the odor of buckskin clothes, she remembered all the old tales like vivid splashes of color on white linen. She forgot her grief instantly, for she was certain she was going to be killed. In that moment of realization, the world about her went out of focus and she fainted.

The Shawnee carried Sarah into the forest and laid her gently on the ground at Jacques Ribalt's feet. Ribalt looked down at the girl and said, "Is she hurt?"

"No, Ribalt," an Indian called Sleeping Wolf said.

Ribalt looked at Jimmy. "Well, there she is, boy. Take a good look at her. You want a woman what faints in the face of trouble?"

Jimmy dropped to his knees, and as if touching a deadly snake, reached out a hand to the fine yellow hair that flowed out from beneath the calico sunbonnet and spilled onto the ground. When he looked up, a fire burned in his black eyes. "I want her, Pa." He could hide his desire no longer. "I want her real bad."

Ribalt laughed. "Well, you're gonna have to wait a while longer. If'n you intend to marry that girl, we better do it up right, or her kin will come and take her away from you, boy."

"What do you mean, do it up right?"

"I mean, you don't take her like a man has a right to take a woman until a preacher marries you two up proper. Once the words are spoke, she becomes your property, and then nobody can take it. And if they try, you'll have to fight for her."

"I will, Pa. I will."

Ribalt laughed again and said, "We'll see. Let's get her back home and lock her up somewhere where she can't run off." He studied the place where Sarah had been kidnapped. He had brought along a Choctaw arrow, acquired once in his travels north. He stalked back to the deadfall, placed the arrow on the ground in plain sight and dropped a swatch of buckskin with glass beadwork stitching beside it. He sent two of the Indians to lay down a false trail while he and Jimmy and the last Indians bore Jimmy's bride through the forest to Ribalt's cabin.

Ribalt took Jimmy aside later. "Your ma ain't real pleased with us taking that girl," he said.

"She ain't gonna make us take her back, is she, Pa?"

"She can't make us do anything," Ribalt said, annoyed at his son for even considering such a thing.

Jimmy felt the emergence of a grin. "She sure is a pretty little thing, ain't she?"

Ribalt didn't think blond hair or blue eyes were particularly attractive. He did think, however, that kidnapping a wife for his son was certain to bring trouble to his doorstep, and he wanted the marriage over with, and his son moved out to deal on his own with a wrathful wife and vengeful in-laws. He said, "Tomorrow morning you ride down to St. Elizabeth and find that preacher man, Daub, and bring him here."

"What should I tell him?"

"I don't care what you tell him, only don't tell him it's to marry you up with that English gal or you'll have the law down around us faster than you can say 'I do.' "

"I wouldn't do that, Pa," Jimmy said, feeling justifiably hurt by his father's low opinion of his cleverness.

Ribalt glanced at the smokehouse where an iron bar wedged through the door handle kept it locked up. "You just get him here, even if you got to bring him by gunpoint. We can't keep her locked up for long. Your ma's already squealing we ought to bring her into the house."

Jimmy laughed and shook his head. "Women," he said. "Where do they get their foolish notions from?"

"Just wait and see, boy. You're about to learn yourself a bellyful about women." Without further words on the matter, he hefted his rifle, slung a sack of traps over his shoulder and left to set out another line.

· · · ·

The next several days McKendree made strides toward regaining his strength. The muscle in his side was stitching itself together nicely, and he had made short journeys afield each day, growing stronger. Carlotta told him, when he had inquired about it, that the footpath up to the ridge line dropped down into another valley beyond, and it was someplace back there that the cave was located, but her father had never taken her to it.

He had cleaned and polished the blunderbuss, and although it was an odd weapon, the more he carried it, the more at home it began to feel in his hands. He and Rudd spent an evening casting up shot for it, and the next day they fired it out across the water to see what sort of pattern it produced.

That evening, Rudd announced he was leaving in the morning on another business trip. McKendree saw the concern in Emma's eyes as Rudd said he'd be gone for two days, and that he would return on Sunday evening.

"Would you like some company?" McKendree asked casually, aware of the look of approval that came to Emma's face.

"Not this time," Gutterie said over the dirty dishes that cluttered the table. "I don't reckon you're well enough to take a trip on the river yet, 'specially if we happen onto rough water."

"But Mr. McKendree is healing up real fine," Emma said.

Rudd gave her a stare that put an end to any more discussion. Emma and Carlotta cleaned up the dishes. Rudd joined McKendree on the bench out front of the house where a setting sun turned the surface of the Missouri River into a slow-moving sheet of blood-red glass.

Duchess came around the corner of the cabin and sat between the two men. McKendree scratched the big dog and said, "I reckon the time has come for me and Duchess to be leaving." He studied the smoke curling from the bowl of his clay pipe, then said, "I never did get you that bear I promised you. Is there anything I can do around here to show you my appreciation before I leave?"

"You owe nothin'. We enjoyed having you around."

McKendree had hoped that Gutterie would ask for his help, but perhaps he really didn't know the danger he and his family were facing. Well, even if Rudd didn't know, he was certain Emma did. He wondered how she could come to know what Rudd's men were planning, and then he recalled Carlotta telling him that her mother often visited with Wilma LaVoie. Had Andre LaVoie told his wife? Had the two women talked?

"When are you leaving?" Gutterie asked.

"Soon."

Gutterie said, "I do have one thing you might do for me, if'n you set in your mind to show us your kindness in return."

McKendree removed his pipe from his lips and looked at Gutterie. "Anything, Rudd," he said.

"I'd appreciate it if you stayed around until I get back Sunday night. You know, just to keep an eye on Emma and Carlotta while I'm gone."

So, he did know something was afoot, even if he didn't know exactly what it was. McKendree had planned to stay that long anyway. He sucked on his pipe and said, "I'll do that for you, Rudd."

Gutterie nodded his head. "Thanks." He stood. "Well, I reckon I'll stroll down and see how the water's moving."

McKendree watched him step out onto the pier where the keelboat was moored. Night came full upon the land. Rudd stayed by the water, in the darkness. After a while, McKendree went inside. Emma was sewing by candlelight. She gave him a smile and offered him a cup of coffee.

McKendree declined the coffee, lay on his bed and folded an arm over his eyes. When he awoke some hours later, the house was dark, and from the back room came the hushed sounds of Emma's and Rudd's voices.

TWENTY-FOUR

"WHAT DO YOU MEAN, pull out and leave? Leave to where?" Rudd Gutterie said.

"I don't know, Rudd. Maybe we could move up the river toward Independence, or beyond. . . ." Emma's low voice carried a worried tone.

"Beyond? Good Lord, woman, there ain't nothing beyond except Indians, and wild country like you ain't never seen before. You know how you worry about Indians!"

"We can go downriver. You could get a job in St. Louis hauling freight."

There was a long pause. McKendree lay in the next room imagining Rudd Gutterie frowning at that suggestion. He heard him say, "St. Louis has got too many people. I'd feel all hemmed in and itchy, like wearing a shirt collar. No, I can't move to St. Louis. And why all of a sudden do you want to move anyway?"

"I just think we've outstayed our welcome here. I think it's a good time to find someplace else. And maybe it's time you find a different sort of work, too," she added pointedly.

There was another pause. "Who have you been talking to, Emma? What's been said?"

"It ain't so much what's been said. It's more the way it's been said. I get the feeling Wilma is trying to put distance between us. As if she knows something she don't want me to know, and she don't want to be too close to me when it comes about. Rudd, what is going on?"

"It's nothing, Emma. The boys are tiptoeing on egg shells because of McKendree, that's all. They're afraid he'll find out about our . . . business dealings."

"Then why don't you get out of it, Rudd? I ain't never been easy with this life we lead, what with you stealing from folks and—"

"Shhhh, woman. You want her to hear?"

"Carlotta is asleep. But that's another thing. How long are we gonna be able to keep on living a lie? How long before Carlotta learns the truth that her father is nothing more than a river pirate!"

As McKendree listened in the darkness, he heard the resolve in Gutterie's voice quaver. McKendree figured Emma was telling him things he'd thought over a time or two himself.

Gutterie said, "We'll talk about this when I get back."

"Why do you have to go at all? We ain't got much here. We could pack it all in the boat and be out of here by tomorrow noon. Mr. McKendree is well enough to be on his own now. He don't need us anymore. We can go someplace new and start over again. You can get honest work, Rudd. We won't never again have to worry about Carlotta finding out the truth."

"Emma, it's too late for me to get honest work on the river. Soon as Finn and Janck found out I was gone, they'd come a looking for me. I'd end up in the river with my throat laid open."

"What you're saying is, there ain't no hope for a new life?"

"I don't know, Emma. I can't think about it now. I'm too tired. I got too much on my brain. We'll talk when I get back."

"If you get back," she said.

Gutterie gave a short laugh. "I'll be back. My men need me. Whatever trouble we're having will blow over once McKendree moves on. You'll see."

For a moment neither of them spoke. McKendree recalled the plans he'd overheard Sculty and LaVoie making. The time had come to tell Gutterie. He'd do it the next morning before Rudd left.

Then he heard Emma say, "Rudd?"

"Mmmm?" came a sleepy reply.

"I was right proud of you for helping Mr. McKendree like you did."

Gutterie laughed softly and said, "I wonder sometimes what came over me."

"Whatever it was," Emma said, "it was a good thing."

"Yeah, well, it sure got me in hot water with the boys. Good night, Emma."

" 'Night, Rudd."

The conversation ceased and in a few minutes the sound of soft snoring filled the quiet house. But McKendree remained awake. He needed sleep. He needed it desperately. Even the small efforts he'd made that day had worn him out. Yet, he remained awake, thinking through what he had heard, planning how he could best help Rudd when the time came. Perhaps once he told him of Sculty's plans, Gutterie would take Emma's advice and strike out for new territory. There were just too many of them for two men to fight alone.

Sleepless nights seemed to be becoming a habit. He lay awake all night, laying out plans in detail, and finally fell into a deep, sound sleep shortly before dawn. A sleep that completely changed all his carefully thought-out plans.

Charles Goodwin searched all day for Sarah. He'd found the arrow in the mud, and the beads, and the trace left behind by the Indians. It led away north and west a short distance and then simply disappeared, as if the Indians who had kidnapped his daughter had sprouted wings and flown away. He returned that evening, blind with worry and fear, to find Rachael at the door with hopeful, tear-swollen eyes.

"You didn't find Sarah?" she said as he stepped past her into the cabin.

"I'm going to St. Elizabeth for the constable," he said, pausing long enough to rip off a piece of bread. Rachael set out a bowl of stew. It remained untouched. Ten minutes later, Charles had his horse saddled. He drew up at the front door where Rachael stood with her fingers digging into Tommy's shoulders.

"Be careful, Charles," she said. "And please hurry."

He swung down and kissed her goodbye. "Keep the door bolted. I'll be back by morning." He wrapped his arms around her. "Try to get some sleep. We'll find her, I promise."

Rachael tried to be brave. She didn't want to send Charles off with tears, but these last several weeks had been too much to bear. They'd lost Noreen, Josiah and Lucas—and now their own daughter. Charles held her for a long moment, then turned and leaped to his horse, leaving a plume of dust rising into the evening sky as he rode hard for St. Elizabeth.

Rachael watched the empty road long after he had ridden from sight, then she hurried Tommy back into the cabin and dropped the heavy timber bar across the door. She shut all of the shutters, barring them tight against the night and its dangers. She stirred up the fire in the hearth and set a single candle on the table. The candle burned down and went out during the night, as did the fire beneath the blackened kettle hanging in the hearth. And while Tommy slept, Rachael sobbed all alone.

Yellow Leaf filled a bowl with potato soup and sliced a wedge of bread, spreading soft lard all over it.

"Where you goin', woman?" Ribalt said as she stepped toward the door.

She stopped and looked at her husband standing in the doorway of the room they slept in. "The girl needs to eat."

"She'll be all right," he said. "I don't want you opening that door without someone near to catch the whelp if she escapes."

"Then you can come with me," she said.

Anger spread swiftly across his face. "I said no!"

Yellow Leaf backed from the doorway. "How many more days must she be locked up?"

"Until I let her out. Now, come here, woman."

Yellow Leaf fought down a cold shiver. She knew what to expect when he called her into the bedroom like that. She had, years earlier, simply tried to ignore his rough touch, and his fierce passion that always turned to violence. But she found she could not. Her forced indifference gradually grew to disgust, and Ribalt sensed it, driving him on to further violence. Refusing him was worse yet. She'd done that too, and he'd beat her in front of the children, driving her naked and bleeding from the cabin.

"Woman!" he said, his impatience flaring.

Yellow Leaf squared her shoulders and stepped stoically forward. Though painful, these interludes never lasted very long. His massive hand folded around the back of her neck and wheeled her to the bed.

Afterward, with Ribalt satisfied, and asleep, Yellow Leaf slipped silently out of bed and went into the other room to gently wash the blood from her body where Ribalt's teeth had broken skin. Then she dressed quietly, opened the door and took the bread and potato soup out to the smokehouse. With some difficulty, she removed the iron bar from the door and swung it open a crack.

"Sarah Goodwin?" she said, cautiously opening the door wider. Moonlight fell through the opening in a band that illuminated the far corner. The little girl huddled back there with wide, terrified eyes watching her.

Yellow Leaf's heart went out to the child, but she was helpless to aid her in any way but to bring her food. If she allowed the girl to leave, Ribalt would beat her, and perhaps kill her. Yellow Leaf paused in her thoughts and considered. Death might be preferable to living with Ribalt. She immediately dismissed the thought. She remembered as a child her father saying that where there is life, there is hope. Yellow Leaf was determined to cling to life and the hope that accompanied it.

"I brought you some food, child," she said, stepping inside.

If it were possible, Sarah would have melded with the wood where she huddled.

"I won't hurt you," Yellow Leaf said, moving closer. She dropped down to put her eyes level with the girl's. "I brought you food," she said. "You need to eat, to keep your strength."

Suddenly the narrow band of light widened. The door slammed open. Yellow Leaf spun about to see Ribalt's huge form framed against the night sky. She could not see his face, only his quivering bulk as his anger swelled up and engulfed him.

"I told you no food!" he rumbled.

Sarah's eyes expanded until all that could be seen of them was white.

"She wasn't going to run away—" Yellow Leaf started to say. Ribalt's hand reached down and caught the material of her dress. He lifted her off the ground and flung her from the smokehouse. The door slammed shut, filling the cramped quarters with darkness.

In the darkness, Sarah began to cry again, while outside she heard the iron bar being driven into place, and then, for a long, horrifying moment, Yellow Leaf's terrified cries filled the air, and the resounding slap of flesh against flesh. Then quite suddenly, the anguished cries stopped.

The deathly quiet that followed was even more terrifying to the fourteen-year-old girl, and she longed to be home, safe on her mother's lap, folded lovingly into her father's strong arms.

TWENTY-FIVE

WHEN HE OPENED HIS EYES, the angle of the sunlight coming through the window brought McKendree totally awake. He threw off the covers and the muscles in his side pulled like stiff leather. Emma was hunched over the table near the hearth, rolling a ball of yellow dough into a broad, flat circle.

"Good morning," she said, trying to sound cheery, but the unhappiness in her voice was clear. "You slept well," she said encouragingly.

"Where's Rudd?" he asked, glancing toward the back room.

"Rudd left about half an hour ago." She paused with her weight still on the handles of the rolling pin. "Why?"

McKendree stepped to the door, where Duchess bounded up the path from the river and planted her paws on his chest. He gave her a pat on the head, then pushed her down, peering along the river to the east, then west. But all he saw was the low profile of a single flatboat across the wide expanse of water.

"Mr. McKendree?" Emma said at his side. He turned to see her staring at him curiously. When she didn't speak at once he said:

"I had something I wanted to tell your husband before he left, that's all."

"Can you tell me?"

He fixed a smile on his face and said, "It's not important, Mrs. Gutterie. I'll speak to Rudd when he gets back. Did he tell you I'll be leaving soon as he returns?"

She studied him a long moment, as if there was something she wanted to say too, then she nodded her head and said, "Rudd told me last night. You'll be going after that man then, Jacques Ribalt?"

McKendree's fists tightened involuntarily at the sound of Ribalt's name. He let them go limp and he said, "Yes, I'll be going after him."

"You're healing quickly, but you're not strong."

"I've been away too long as it is."

She nodded her head as if she understood his urgency. "I best get back to work," she said, turning to the cabin.

"Mrs. Gutterie?"

"Yes?"

"What time Sunday do you expect Rudd back?"

"He said evening."

"Will he be going to the cave first?"

She stiffened in the doorway, grasping the jamb. "How do you know about that?"

He shrugged his shoulders. "I reckon Rudd must have mentioned it when we were talking."

She said, "Yes, I suppose he will go there first."

McKendree's lips drew together in a thoughtful frown. "You know, I'm feeling right spry this morning, Mrs. Gutterie. I think I'll just gather me together some supplies and see if I can't get that bear I promised Rudd."

Emma eased her grip on the door frame. "Rudd told you that ain't necessary."

"I know, but a long walk will do me admirably this morning, and if'n I'm out tracing about the woods, anyway, I might just as well be hunting, don't you think?"

"How will you bring it back?" she asked. "You're not strong enough to haul a bear down out of the woods."

"I'll quarter it and haul it back in pieces."

The look of concern eased into a smile, but it was plain a worrisome thought still nudged at her. "I'll pack you something to eat along the way."

Carlotta was on the floor in the sunlight coming through the window, playing with a rag doll she called Amelia. She smiled at him when he entered and said, "Papa was real quiet not to wake you, Mr. McKendree."

He grinned. "Your pa did a right proud job of it."

Carlotta smiled and said, "Where you going?"

"Out to catch us a bear to eat." He hefted the blunderbuss and looked at it. "I might just bring back two or three if I'm not careful."

Carlotta giggled. She said to Amelia, "Say goodbye to Mr. McKendree," and waved the doll's arm.

Emma prepared a sack of food. "You don't really expect to hit anything with that ancient thing, do you?"

"With the spread this gun puts out, I don't expect I can hardly miss, so long as the critter's not standing any farther away than that front door."

She put the sack in his hand. "You be careful. Remember, you're shy yet three weeks of healing."

"I'll be careful," he said. "I'll be back this afternoon."

McKendree put on his hat and stepped outside. Duchess fell in at his heels as he started along the trace to Reese Sculty's cabin. Once beyond the sight of Gutterie's cabin, he doubled back to the footpath that climbed up to the ridge top. Carlotta had said the cave was somewhere in the valley beyond. Well, if this was the trace Rudd and his men took to and from the cave, he'd have no difficulty finding it.

As the land rose, that familiar pain in his side returned—more an annoyance now than the debilitating ache it had been less than a week ago. He pushed on, ignoring it, and when he reached the top of the ridge he sat upon a boulder and carefully loaded the blunderbuss, pouring in a measure of powder, an oversized patch and a full twenty-count of fifty-caliber balls. He topped it off with a cotton-ticking patch and primed the pan.

Duchess rooted around a badger hole awhile as he worked. She spun about instantly when McKendree called to her, and bounded out ahead of him. This part of the walk was mostly downhill. McKendree covered it with a brisk stride, the ache no more than a dull throb. The trace was well-worn, and a mile farther east, it branched to the north. Here the heavy traffic seemed to turn off. McKendree set his moccasins on this new trace and in a few minutes was winding through a narrow limestone ravine.

He came around an outcropping and dropped to one knee, putting a restraining hand on Duchess. "Sit, girl," he whispered. Beyond the fringe of trees a broad clearing opened up, and a wide footpath led down to the river where a rickety pier stretched out into the water. He studied the terrain which climbed mostly straight up around him. There seemed to be no one about. His eyes moved to the black hole in the side of the rocks. When he looked back at Duchess, she was wagging her tail.

"Let's take a closer look at this," he said, and as if she had understood him perfectly, she stood and ran ahead, putting her nose to the ground by the mouth of the cave and turning a half-dozen circles. She trotted down to the river for a drink.

McKendree viewed the dark mouth of the cave a moment, and studied the rock face around it. High up the cliff the neck of a whiskey bottle protruded from a cleft in the rocks. On the ground below, shards of glass littered the foot-packed earth. McKendree hunkered down and extracted the bottle label from the shards. A faint grin tugged at the corner of his mouth as he recalled the bottle he and Rudd had shared.

He stepped into the cave, where a rough, wooden wall and a padlocked door barred his way. Beyond the cracks in the wood planking a passageway continued into the darkness. McKendree tugged at the lock. It was solid. He could blast it open with the blunderbuss, but he dismissed that idea immediately, stepping back into the daylight. There's no reason to show your hand before it's time to lay down your cards, he thought wryly.

Down on the pier, newly chafed wood told him several boats had been tied up to it recently. As he walked out onto it, Duchess came along the river bank and pranced up to his side. McKendree watched the slow waters move through the pilings. Waters that were rapidly becoming a life-giving artery to the West—*the Great Western Wilderness,* as George Winfield's advertisement had called it—and somewhere upon these waters was Rudd Gutterie . . . and a band of river pirates that meant him no earthly good.

Rudd Gutterie hugged the long rudder shaft under his arm as the tree-covered shoreline moved past him. From his vantage point atop the cabin, he could see the changing river far ahead. Reese Sculty stood at the bow, and Soute and Bensen were stationed port and starboard with fending poles in hand. But the river was broad and deep here, and there was little to imperil their journey.

A mile west of the town of Hermann, Rudd put the boat over. Six men leaped off her gunnels and waded ashore, holding their guns and powder above their heads. Reese Sculty led the landing party. Andre LaVoie splashed out of the water behind him, along with Jim Candelass and "Sneaky" Bill Cutter of Finn Johnson's boat. Gabe Piper and Tully de Grosse, both of Janck Hennigan's crew, were with them. Once ashore, they dove into the tree cover that grew down to the water's edge and made for the docks at Hermann, and the side-wheeler *Morning Glory*.

Rudd Gutterie shouted the command to push out once the landing party was out of sight. His men thrust their poling staffs into the muddy river bottom and shoved the boat back into the current. Gutterie ordered the sail hoisted to take advantage of a westerly wind, and for the rest of the day they muscled the little keelboat up the river.

An hour after sunset the *Gutt's Bucket* tied up in a cove beyond Sandy Hook where the *Deborra* and the *Beaver Tail* were waiting. Gutterie's men wasted no time clambering ashore through the cold water. A campfire was burning on the bank. Gutterie paused upon the dark deck to watch them leave. Inside the cabin, a feeble candle burned. A shadow moved across its light.

"You comin' ashore, Rudd?"

Gutterie turned to see Elliot Soute watching him. Soute carried a corked bottle of whiskey in his hand, and of all the crew, he had been the only member to remain sober. His arm hugged a rifle, and a hunting bag hung over his shoulder. "You gonna get drunk now, Elliot?"

A faint smile moved across his face, then it disappeared. "I might have me a sip or two," he said. "I'm mainly bringing this along for the boys. Coming? It's still hours before the *Morning Glory* is due. Sculty will sound her whistle to let us know."

"I'll be along in a while, Elliot."

Soute nodded his head at the pistol tucked under Gutterie's belt. "You might want to keep that thing handy."

Gutterie narrowed an eye. "You think I might have need of it, Elliot?"

"Never can tell."

"According to the *Morning Glory's* manifest, all she's a carryin' is cargo. No passengers scheduled. Sculty and the boys will put the crew off downriver before they get this far. I shouldn't have any need of this here pistol if all goes to plan."

Soute shrugged his shoulders. "Then let's hope everything goes to plan, Rudd." He grinned and lowered himself over the boat's gunnels. Standing waist deep in the water, he looked back. "But just the same, Rudd, be careful."

Elliot waded ashore to join the others. In the darkness, Rudd Gutterie pondered Elliot's words and wondered if there might be more going on here than he was willing to admit. He'd recognized a distinct coolness among his men on the voyage upriver, but there had been a bitter controversy over McKendree; a coolness was understandable. McKendree would be leaving in a day or two and things would get back to normal. Even Emma would see that her worries had been for nothing.

These thoughts reassured him, but just the same, he was grateful McKendree had agreed to stay and keep an eye on Emma and Carlotta until he returned, and just the same . . . He patted the pistol beneath his belt. Its presence eased that little bit of uncertainty he couldn't quite shake.

Gutterie joined his men ashore. The drinking was heavy and serious, and neither Janck nor Finn seemed inclined to curb their men's appetites. Gutterie stayed clear of the bottle, drinking coffee instead —and so, he noticed, did Elliot.

At quarter past eleven the distant, lonely whistle of the *Morning Glory* echoed across the black water. The men made their way down to the shoreline as the riverboat's forward running lanterns broke clear of the trees and shone around the bend in the river. Then she came into view, her twin wheels churning under a full head of steam, driving the long, graceful boat straight for the sandbars of Sandy Hook.

TWENTY-SIX

McKENDREE ROLLED A SHEET of newspaper into a tube and twisted one end of it shut. "Pardon me for saying so, ma'am," he said as he worked, "but frowning doesn't become you."

Emma Gutterie put down her needle and thread and looked across the room at him. "I've things on my mind, Mr. McKendree," she said.

"You're worried about the problems Rudd's been having because of me."

"How did you know that?"

McKendree set the paper tube aside and began forming a second one. "I was awake last night when you two were talking about it. I didn't mean to overhear, but I couldn't very well help it."

She ceased her rocking in the high-back chair. The rhythmic squeaking stopped and an unnatural silence filled the cabin. For a second she sat there staring at him. "Then you know?"

"You mean about what Rudd does? Who his 'business' partners are? I've known that for some time. I've suspected it even longer."

"What are you going to do about it?" she asked cautiously.

A lamp on a shelf above Emma's right shoulder gave light to her stitching, and a candle in front of McKendree illuminated a circle of table top where he was forming sheets of newsprint into paper tubes. "I'm not going to tell the authorities, if that's what you are concerned about, and I'm not going to mention it to Carlotta either," he said. "I don't approve of river piracy, Mrs. Gutterie, but turning Rudd in would be mighty poor payment for the kindness you've shown me."

She continued to stare at him. If his words had put her mind to ease any, she didn't show it. He said, "But I do believe Rudd is in peril because of that kindness, and I intend to help him."

Emma's eyes widened. "Then it's true. His men are planning violence against him."

"Yes, ma'am. I'm afraid it is true."

"That's what you wanted to tell him this morning?"

McKendree nodded his head.

"What are we to do?" she said all at once.

McKendree went to the fireplace, where an iron pot sat on a bed of coals. He stirred the molten lead there with a long-handled dipper and began to ladle it into a four-chamber bullet mold.

Emma put her stitching aside and stood, looking out the window at moonlight upon the slow water. "I must do something," she said finally.

McKendree continued to cast bullets until the tin can at his side was filled with shiny lead balls. "I think the best thing is for you and your daughter to go somewhere. Have you relatives nearby you can stay with?"

"I'm not leaving Rudd to fight this all alone, Mr. McKendree," she said, turning back.

"He won't be alone, Mrs. Gutterie." McKendree carried the bucket of fresh-cast fifty-caliber bullets to the table. "I'll be with him."

"You? How can one man, or even two, fight so many?"

McKendree grinned faintly in the shadows beyond the reach of the candlelight. "It won't be just me, ma'am," he said, counting the bullets out into groups of twenty. "Duchess is worth at least three strong men."

"But there will be twenty against you."

He glanced at the blunderbuss resting on the edge of the table and his grin broadened. "I still got me an elf in the woodpile that I reckon will come as a big surprise to those twenty men," he said as he carefully filled each tube with bullets and twisted the ends into a compact package.

Jimmy Ribalt didn't find Reverend Daub in St. Elizabeth, but while there he heard the news spreading through the town of the child who had been taken by a band of Choctaws. What Choctaws were doing this far west, no one could say, but the men formed a search party at once, and the women fixed a basket of bread and meat to send along.

They were now three days on the trail—a trail that went nowhere. Jimmy Ribalt smiled at the thought of all those men riding off in the wrong direction.

Upon inquiring, the farrier told him that Reverend Daub was at a town called Clement Creek. Jimmy rode hard and made Clement Creek as the sun was going down. He found Daub coming out of the mercantile store.

"Daub," he said, reining his horse to a stop.

Russell Daub came to a halt in the middle of the street and pushed his spectacles up the bridge of his nose. "Yes?" he said, and then he recognized the boy. "You're Jimmy Ribalt."

"Yes, sir."

"What is it you want?" he said brusquely, remembering the ignoble treatment he had received in times past at the Ribalt cabin. Almost at once he caught himself in these un-Christian feelings and chided himself for succumbing to the sin of pride. He said, "I'm sorry. How can I help you?"

"My pa sent me to find you. He wants to see you right quick."

"Your father? He wants to see me?" Daub could not have been more surprised if an emissary of the Southern Nations had told him that all the chiefs there were requesting a Christmas service. Daub stammered. "What possibly could your father want with me?"

Jimmy grinned. "Pa's gone and found the Lord. He wants to be baptized."

That rocked Daub back on his heels. He recovered a moment before tumbling all the way over. "Glory be," he said, barely above a whisper.

"So, can you come?" Jimmy urged.

"Ah, certainly. I am finished here. I was going to St. Elizabeth in the morning, but yes, I can come." His thoughts were jumbled. Ribalt was the last man on earth he expected a summons from, and certainly never for the reason Jimmy gave. "Just let me get my things together."

"All right, Reverend, but Pa's in a real big hurry. He figures he's got a lot of sinning to be cleaned of in his life."

"I reckon he does," Daub said, still in a daze.

Daub packed his gear, said goodbye to the family he was staying with in Clement Creek, and an hour later, with night stretching across the land, they were on their way.

Jimmy was about to bust his buttons. He'd gotten Daub to come with him never having to poke his rifle in the preacher's ribs even once. He expanded his chest as they rode. In two days, maybe three, Sarah Goodwin would be his wife. Then no one would take her from him, not another man, not her parents . . . not unless they wanted to face his gun.

The search for Sarah Goodwin became at once a massive effort of men and horses, but after the first day, everyone but Charles and Rachael knew the girl was not going to be found. Still, for the Goodwins' sake, they pressed on until one by one the men drifted home, to the business of running their own lives, of caring for their own wives and daughters.

Charles Goodwin kept on. Alone, but there was no place left to look. His only lead lay in the Choctaw arrow. Yet no one had seen any Indians in the area, let alone Choctaws. His only hope of finding Sarah was to travel himself to the Choctaw nations and pick up his search there.

He rode up to his cabin after sunset and swung off his horse. "Rachael?" he called when she hadn't appeared at the sound of his approach. She had always been immediately at the door. Now the open doorway was empty. Charles Goodwin came immediately alert. "Tommy!"

"In here, Pa!" Tommy said with an urgency that impelled Charles forward. Goodwin stopped just inside the bedroom doorway and looked down at the bed where his wife lay.

"Rachael," he said, dropping beside the bed. She didn't speak. He wasn't sure she had even heard him. Sweat glistened on her face, and the pillow beneath her hair was damp. He placed a hand on her forehead and felt the heat.

"How long has your mother been like this?"

"I don't know, Pa. Most of the day. She said she didn't feel well this morning. I was outside awhile and when I came in she was asleep."

"Your ma's not asleep. She's burning up with fever. It's the worry sickness," he said, nodding his head at the bucket of water on the floor and the damp cloth in Tommy's hand. "You done right trying to cool her, son. I'll take over now." Goodwin pulled a chair around. "Get yourself something to eat and bring me whatever you can find." For the rest of the night he tenderly bathed the fever, but by morning, Rachael Goodwin's condition had not improved.

TWENTY-SEVEN

McKENDREE LEFT EARLY the following morning, carrying the blunderbuss over his shoulder on a sling he'd fashioned from an old harness, and the rifle he'd taken from Reese Sculty's cabin. The hunting bag sagged off his shoulder with the weight of the extra lead and powder, and he carried a second horn of powder across his other shoulder to help balance it out.

His brisk pace slowed as the land rose, but he pushed on. It would be a long time before he would regain his full strength, but he felt stronger today than he had in weeks, and he couldn't permit the growing ache in his side to keep him from arriving at the cave before Rudd and his river pirate companions returned. Atop the ridge he paused to catch his breath. Duchess brushed a patch of ground clear of yellow-gold leaves with her tail until the pain subsided and he was on his way again. It was still morning when he eased himself through the narrow cut in the limestone cliffs and found a place where he had a view of the clearing below, and the river to his left.

McKendree laid out the guns, shot and powder in a fashion that would put them near at hand. A fall breeze coming off the water made him shiver where he lay hidden in the shade behind a cairn of boulders. Fall already! He wondered about the exact date, and discovered he'd even lost track of the month. It had been—how long? Three weeks. It might already be October. Noreen's birthday was the tenth of October. Perhaps he had missed that, too.

He examined one of the shot-filled tubes he'd constructed the night before. The date he found on it was July 16. The paper had already been two months old when all this had begun—two months. How different his life had been such a short time ago. His biggest concern then was keeping the weeds from strangling the growing corn that his muscles and sweat had put in that spring. Corn that by now was ready to harvest. And here he was, lying in cover, waiting for returning river pirates . . . grieving for a dead son . . . not knowing if the wife he loved would be waiting for him when he returned. How could his life have changed course so quickly?

McKendree blinked away the moisture growing, unwanted, in his eyes and packed the bowl of his pipe with the tobacco Rudd had given him. He wasn't a philosopher, he told himself, although Noreen sometimes accused him of that. He was a farmer. Or at least he had been a farmer, he thought wryly, glancing at the blunder- buss resting atop the hunting bag. "Odd tools for a farmer to be using," he commented dryly.

He cast about and found Duchess up the hillside, lying in a patch of sunshine coming through the trees. "You've got the right idea, girl," he said, groaning softly as he stood. The land higher up gave him a broader picture of the river. He eased himself down next to the dog and felt the sun drive the chill from his body. Duchess was a comfort just to be near. He figured that was because right now, she was the only link he had to a time that had been happier.

The morning wore on and the sun grew stronger as it moved straight overhead. McKendree went down to his supplies and opened a bag Emma had handed him before he left. Fried catfish, corn bread, raspberry tart. He ate his fill. Duchess wandered off to find her own lunch.

The traffic along the river had been light all morning. It was along about two o'clock that he noticed the three specks on the water far to the west. McKendree watched them grow larger and take on the shape of keelboats. He knew a surge of vitality as they veered off their course and angled across the current toward the pier.

From his place out of sight, he watched the boats tie up. Faded white paint on the cabin of the boat nearest him read *Deborra*. The *Beaver Tail* and the *Gutt's Bucket* tied up on the far side of the pier.

Rudd Gutterie stepped off his boat and began to shout orders to his men. Barrels of flour and unmarked crates were carried off the three boats and hauled into the cave. Just within view to his right, the door to the cave stood open, and a line of torches set into the wall illuminated a passageway that bent beyond his sight. Next, bolts of cloth emerged from the boats to disappear into the cave on the shoulders of the men.

McKendree recognized Reese Sculty and Andre LaVoie among the men that bustled about like ants. He picked out Finn and Janck too. They mostly shouted orders and did mighty little carrying. McKendree settled back to patiently wait out the long process of unloading the stores of what must have been a wealthy shipper. In the end, the men began to off-load small barrels in bucket-brigade fashion. The casks emerged from the wooden bellies of the boats one after another until the dock stood shoulder high with them. The markings on the barrels were plain enough.

Gunpowder—enough to supply a small army. McKendree whistled softly and figured a man could get rich on this alone, not even counting the flour and trade goods that had already made their way into the cave. No wonder the sturdy door and iron padlock.

The barrels continued coming until only a narrow passage between them was left for the men to squeeze past.

Then the sounds of voices drew his eye from the growing stack of gunpowder to the mouth of the cave. It was Gutterie he heard first. Rudd was standing with Finn and Janck, and two other men McKendree did not recognize. "What are you talking about, Finn?" he said loud enough to not only draw McKendree's attention, but to turn the heads of the men just finishing transferring the powder casks to the dock.

"I'm talking about us parting company, old friend," Finn said. McKendree looked at the man speaking. He was taller than Gutterie, but half as wide. His hair was coarse and black, and he spoke in a dialect McKendree had never heard before. He tried to put a name to it, and couldn't, but something at the back of his brain made him think of Louisiana.

"What's wrong, Finn? Ain't happy with the way I pull my weight around here?" Gutterie said.

"It ain't that, Rudd," another man that McKendree figured to be Janck Hennigan said.

"Then what?"

Finn said, "Got a pretty operation goin' here. Good money for everyone. But fer we to keep goin' like we is, us gotta keep our secret to us-selves. Now what you went and done, Rudd, that done put us all in jeopardy. Me an' the boys, us talk mighty hard on it. Us think that m'be you ain't reliable no more."

"What are you talking about, Finn?" Gutterie narrowed an eye at the taller man. "It's McKendree, ain't it? You don't think I'd tell him anything?"

Reese Sculty shouldered into the crowd and placed himself at Finn's elbow.

Finn said, "You don't have to tell someb'dy for them to figure it out."

"Well, he didn't, and he won't. Besides, tomorrow he's leavin'. Our secret is safe—"

"For the time being, Rudd," Sculty said.

Gutterie pinned him back with a stare and said, "What is that I'm hearing in your voice, Reese?"

Sculty held his ground. "I'm throwing in with Finn."

"I should have figured if anyone was going to make trouble, it was going to be you, Reese. Well, go on, and good riddance to you."

There followed a shift of the men. Gutterie watched his crew move over to throw support to Finn. He said, "I seem to have a mutiny on my hands."

"M'be this time us got offa the hook, Rudd, but us figures somethin's come over you for pullin' that sorry feller outa the river in the first place. M'be you will pull another sorry feller outa the river next month. M'be that sorry feller will find out about we. So, us figure it time to cut our lines."

Gutterie stepped backward into a man standing there with his arms crossed. "What exactly do you mean, cut lines?"

Finn grinned. "Us gotta spell it plain out for you?"

Gutterie's hand moved for the pistol under his belt. Someone grabbed his arm and another yanked the pistol free and handed it over to Finn Johnson.

"Okay, I spell it plain out for you, Rudd. Us gonna kill you here and now. Cut out the weak link. Then us figures Reese will take your boat. Three boats make us work more easy."

"How do you think you'll get away with that? My boat is known around these parts. My wife will—" Gutterie stopped suddenly, realizing the damage his words could cause.

Finn said, "Us take care of you wife and chil' too, Rudd. Don't worry," he grinned, "you three be all together."

"You can't do that, Finn. . . . Janck?" For the first time McKendree saw panic in Gutterie's face. "Kill me if you must, but not my family."

Reese said, "Like you said, she'd have the authorities breathing down our necks in a minute."

"But—" Rudd started, and then gulped back his words. Finn raised the pistol and drew back the heavy hammer. . . .

McKendree figured this had gone far enough.

TWENTY-EIGHT

McKENDREE STOOD from behind the pile of boulders and put the rifle to his shoulder. "Drop the pistol, Finn," he said, drawing a bead.

Finn Johnson's head came about. The others looked at McKendree too. In the sudden quiet that settled over the men McKendree heard Gutterie breathe, "Thank God."

"Who is you, man?"

"The sorry fellow Rudd fished from the river."

A low muttering ran through the men. Finn kept the pistol pointed at Gutterie, but his full attention was directed at McKendree. "I know'd you'd be trouble to we, McKendree. Why ain't you home in bed where a sick man belong?"

"I figured a walk would be good for my health. As it turns out, it was good for Rudd's health too. I already said it once, but maybe you didn't hear me so I'll say it again, then I'm going to pull this trigger. Put down the gun."

Finn hesitated, but he could see that McKendree meant to shoot, and even if the odds were stacked against this bold stranger, Finn knew the chances were good he'd not survive either. He lowered the pistol, but he did not drop it. He said, "Hey, mister. You only one man, alone. How you expect to stop we?"

"Well, Finn, I sort of figured you for the sensible sort who doesn't want to go through life with a hole in his forehead."

Finn chuckled.

"But the fact of the matter is, I'm not alone."

"Oh? I see nob'dy whit you, McKendree."

"Duchess," he said sharply. The dog trotted out into the clearing and sat down. She stared hungrily at the men with her ears plastered back, and her tail straight out and still as a dead snake.

"So, okay. You got a pup'y dog whit you. That still only counts up to two."

"Make that three." A man stepped clear of the casks of gunpowder on the dock and put a rifle to his shoulder.

McKendree hadn't expected help, but he welcomed all that he could get.

"Elliot!" Gutterie said. "I knew I could count on you."

"Elliot, you make big, bad mistake."

"Maybe, Finn, but I'm sticking with Rudd."

"What will it be, Finn?" McKendree said. "Give up Gutterie, or do we do it the hard way?"

"I think m'be I have no choice now, McKendree." Finn grinned, then brought the pistol up suddenly and fired. The bullet split a chunk of rock from the boulder McKendree was standing behind and in the next instant men were scrambling everywhere. He lost Finn from his sights. Another shot rang out.

McKendree dropped behind the rocks and thrust the rifle over the top of them. In the confusion, Duchess sank her teeth into the leg of one of the fleeing pirates and thrashed her head back like a fish snagged on a hook. McKendree caught a glimpse of Finn, Janck and some of the others sprinting for the cave. He swung toward them and fired as Finn dove out of sight.

Men leaped for cover and gunfire erupted from several places at once. Gutterie long-legged it toward the boulders where McKendree lay and scrambled over the top of them.

"Man, am I glad to see you," he said, hitching himself up close to the rocks.

"Figured you would be. I couldn't get that bear I promised, so I guess this will have to do."

"Consider any debt paid up in full, McKendree."

McKendree grinned and pushed the rifle into Rudd's hands. "Load this thing." He snatched up the blunderbuss and peered over the rocks.

A volley of rifle fire drove his head back down.

"You see Elliot anywhere?" Gutterie asked, ramming a charge down the barrel.

"Last I saw of him, he was by the pier."

Gutterie frowned and shook his head. "Not a good place to be."

"Considering that mountain of powder, no place around here is a good place to be." McKendree chanced another look, swung the blunderbuss toward some nearby trees and fired. Vegetation ripped apart and two men tumbled out and sprawled across the ground.

Gutterie pulled his head back behind the rocks and said, "Elliot is still among the powder kegs, McKendree. I'm going after him."

"I'll give you cover." McKendree filled the short cannon with a packet of shot and rammed a patch over it. "All right, go."

Gutterie lowered his head and leaped into the open. McKendree eyed a stand of trees where rifle fire was coming from and peppered two dozen square feet of it with a single shot. The shooting from that quarter ceased. As he reloaded, Duchess came back wearing a red moustache.

He rammed another packet of shot down the short barrel. Movement at the mouth of the cave drew his next shot. The rock face appeared to disintegrate in a cloud of dust, and when the dust had cleared another man lay dead.

Gutterie made it to Elliot's side. A shot took off the edge of a cask sitting there. McKendree's teeth grated as he hammered another round into the blunderbuss. He had no idea if a stray bullet would set off all that powder, and he didn't want to find out. He eased back into the trees, working his way to higher ground. Most of the pirates had fled, but he knew that Finn and Janck had taken cover in the cave a moment before the shooting began.

Some scattered shots came from the clearing as he made his way around to the cave and dropped down beside it, turning inside. Torches lighted the tunnel back beyond a bend where McKendree could not see. The shooting outside stopped and in another minute Rudd and Elliot stepped into the cave.

"They seem to have scattered to the four winds," Gutterie said, breathing hard.

Elliot glanced at the short, wicked weapon in McKendree's fist and said, "They were outgunned."

"Compliments of Rudd," McKendree said. "Thanks for sticking your neck in this."

"I didn't like the odds," he said, grinning.

"What are we doing now?" Gutterie said.

"Finn and Janck and a few others ducked inside here as the shooting started. Are there any weapons back there?"

"Sure, lots. The place is full of guns."

"That's not going to make this any easier." McKendree stepped through the doorway and slid up against the wall. Gutterie and Soute scurried through and moved to the other side of the passageway. Ahead, the tunnel opened up. McKendree caught a glimpse of the wooden crates and the flour barrels stacked up back there. A man could hide real good behind all that, he figured, cautiously advancing.

A shot echoed inside the cave, driving him back against the wall. He waited a second, then wheeled out in a crouch and fired the blunderbuss. A cloud of flour billowed and obscured everything like a morning fog. They dove under its cover and flattened behind barrels of flour.

McKendree motioned Gutterie and Soute to move out in opposite directions, and hurriedly reloaded his gun. For a moment all was silent. Then he heard the gentle scuffing sounds of someone moving about. In the flames of the torches along the walls, flour dust sputtered and burned as it slowly settled, covering everything with a fine white powder. Something nudged his side, and suddenly Duchess' head was under his hand.

"Good girl," he whispered.

A sound overhead riveted his attention. He glanced up and rolled aside as a barrel of flour crashed to the floor and broke apart. A gunshot rang out. In another part of the cave someone grunted. A target darted past the flurry of white dust and fled out of the cave before McKendree could bring his gun around.

"McKendree! Can you hear my voice?"

"I hear you, Finn."

"I got me Mr. Soute. Him bad hurt. You want him back, you let we pass."

The next moment Gutterie was at his elbow. "He's telling the truth. I saw Elliot get it."

"They live in your back yard, Rudd. Want to let them leave?"

"Not particularly, but I owe Elliot."

"Okay. Finn! Better hightail it before I change my mind."

A shape moved in the dust and then Finn stepped clear, holding Elliot about the waist with a gun to his head.

Elliot was bleeding from the chest, but he was conscious. Gutterie said, "Leave him and get out of here."

"Once us clear of here I leave him." He stood there while Janck and six men moved past McKendree's gun. Then Finn backed out with Soute between him and McKendree. At the pier he waited while his men untied the *Deborra* and the *Beaver Tail*.

They put poles in the water and the boats eased away from the dock. Finn said, "McKendree. I tell you the truth. This meeting is no pleasure for me. I will see you no more, and that is to me all happiness. But Rudd, us will see one another again, and when us do, you will have nob'dy to steal you away from my gun. For now, goodbye." Finn pressed the pistol against Soute's head and pulled the trigger.

"Damn you, Finn!" Gutterie cried as Soute fell to the ground. He threw the rifle to his shoulder and fired. The bullet missed as Finn leaped across six feet of water to the *Deborra*'s deck.

Gunfire drove McKendree and Gutterie back into the cave.

"The bastard killed Elliot. I can't let him get away," Gutterie said.

McKendree had only one shot, and already the boats were moving out beyond the range of the little gun. He twisted one of the torches from the cave's wall and ran out of the cave. A bullet whistled past his ear. He heaved back and threw the torch into the mountain of gunpowder. It landed atop a wooden cask and simply burned harmlessly as the boats pulled away.

"No good," Gutterie said, coming up beside him.

"Get back inside the cave," McKendree said. He shoved Rudd back and put the blunderbuss to his shoulder, taking aim at the torch. The gun fired and almost instantly the pier disintegrated in an orange plume of fire. The concussion picked McKendree up as he dove back into the cave and threw him through the doorway. He landed in a crumpled pile beyond, and lay there a moment, stunned. Slowly he picked himself up. "Rudd?"

From beyond the doorway came a groan, and then Gutterie's face appeared in the rectangle of light. "You're still alive, McKendree?"

"So it would appear."

"Owww, my head hurts."

McKendree stepped outside. The clearing was engulfed in a thick black cloud, and as if a thunderstorm had passed by, everything was soaked, and the ground was mud.

"Did they get away?" Gutterie asked, coming up beside him.

McKendree pointed at where the pier had once stood. Only a few twisted pilings remained. Rudd's boat was half thrown up on the bank, twisted and shattered like a toy stepped on. Farther out in the river, a second boat was slowly heeling over, its splintered wooden planks standing up in the air like giant broken ribs. No sign of Finn's boat could be seen save its broken mast standing two feet out of the water. Elliot was gone too.

"They didn't," McKendree said.

Janck's boat sank into the river and flotsam washed ashore. Duchess sniffed at the wreckage. McKendree found the blunderbuss in the low branches of a tree. They stood there awhile as if expecting something to happen, but nothing ever did. Sore, and tired, they started back to Rudd's cabin.

Emma saw them while they were still some distance off. She ran from the house into Rudd's arms. McKendree stood back, as if restrained by an unseen hand, and as Rudd and Emma held each other he prayed that there would be somebody to greet him and hold him when he returned.

TWENTY-NINE

"WHAT WILL YOU DO NOW?" McKendree asked the next morning. Below, the morning sun sparkled upon the slow river and this day felt to him a little like the opening of a new book, only the old book hadn't quite been finished . . . at least not for him. But the covers had been shut permanently for Rudd Gutterie and his family, and McKendree wondered what would come of these new friends.

"Emma and me, we talked it over last night. We figure it's time for a fresh start. Emma says St. Louis would suit her right fine, but it's a might too civilized for my liking." He looked at his wife standing beside him. McKendree saw the squeeze her arm wrapped about his waist gave him.

McKendree nodded his head to the west where the river disappeared around the bend. "Lots of opportunity out there."

Emma said, "We thought a trading post upriver might turn a profit, and be a respectable profession for Rudd to work at. Once out of here, Rudd is going to send a letter to the Masterson Steamboat Line and tell them where they can find their goods."

McKendree glanced at the pier. No keelboat rocked gently beside it this morning, only the small skiff. "Will you get another boat?"

"Eventually. When I can afford one," Gutterie said. "I reckon I'll miss the feel of a rolling deck beneath my feet before too long."

McKendree extended his hand. "Good luck, then." He dropped the blunderbuss off his shoulder and handed it back.

Rudd shook his head and pushed the gun away. "It's yours. You'll have more need of it now than I will."

McKendree figured no truer words had ever been spoken. He thought of Jacques Ribalt, and the debt Ribalt owed him, a debt too great to ever be repaid.

Emma touched his arm. "Please be careful, Mr. McKendree. We will be thinking about you. I pray you will find your Noreen well and waiting for you when you have finished what it is you have to do."

Something caught in McKendree's throat. He swallowed it down and said, "I appreciate your concern. Thanks."

Carlotta came up the footpath from the river. Her smiling face seemed to say she knew something exciting was about to grab hold of her family and impel them out of this little valley. She had sensed her mother's unhappiness, and her father's dark secret for so long.

"You leaving us today, Mr. McKendree?" Her blue eyes sparkled and the ends of her long hair were teased by the breeze coming off the river.

"Yep. Time's come for me to move on."

Carlotta hesitated with her hand behind her back, then she thrust it out at him with water still dripping between her clenched fingers. "These are for you," she said, averting her eyes and sidling up to her father's leg.

"Indian jewels!" He held the glistening rocks in the sunlight. "Thank you, Carlotta. I'll keep them in my pocket, and whenever I look at them I will remember you."

Carlotta blushed. "All you got to do is get them wet again. Then they will always be pretty and magical."

He tucked them into his shirt pocket. Emma kissed his cheek and Rudd clasped his hand mightily. When he was gone they took themselves back into the cabin and made preparations for their long journey.

There was no deviating from his goal now. McKendree took a bearing on the ridge top and dove into the forest, staying compass-true to his course. His side hurt less and less as the miles melted behind him, and after six hours of walking, the ache seemed to disappear completely. That night he shot an opossum with Reese Sculty's rifle and ate his fill, drinking spring water from a seep.

Watching the small campfire afterward, McKendree made his

plans. He carefully took himself through each step and each time
the plan took a different twist, but the ending was always the same.
Duchess rested her head on his lap and he stroked the large yellow-
fur head as he contemplated the smoke curling from his pipe. Tomorrow, he thought, tomorrow Ribalt would answer for all he had
done.

McKendree worked it out every way. He accounted for all
possibilities. Little did he realize how far he had misjudged
what he would find when he arrived at Ribalt's homestead the
next day.

"I will not perform this travesty against God and the laws
of civilized man!" Reverend Russell Daub said again, and
again, Jacques Ribalt's fist came around and knocked him to
the floor.

Daub hitched himself up on one elbow and wiped blood from his
mouth. Ribalt hovered over him, legs spread, fists clenched and a
wild frenzy turning his bearded face into a caricature of all that
Daub believed to be evil.

"You'll not leave here alive if you don't, preacher man." Ribalt
hooked a hand under Daub's arm and heaved him up into a chair.
He tied his hands to the chair and said, "I'll be back. Meantime,
you think about what I'm gonna do to you if'n you don't come
around, Daub." Ribalt looked at Yellow Leaf huddled back out of
his way. "You don't go coddling him, woman, or you won't get off
so easy next time."

She didn't speak. She couldn't. Her lips were swollen and twisted,
and her left eye had turned black and had closed up. She hugged
her left arm to her waist where it rested in a sling. Antoine had
helped her set the bone, and Louis had taken to clinging to her
skirts now whenever Ribalt was near, further infuriating his father.
Only Jimmy had seemed not to notice her pain.

After he had gone, Yellow Leaf sat down at the table and looked
at the blood drying in the creases of Daub's chin. She dared not
bathe his injuries, or even offer words of sympathy. She dared not
disobey Ribalt again, for like Daub, she knew the next time he
would not hesitate to kill her.

In the morning Jimmy readied himself for the marriage. Ribalt told Daub that today he'd perform the service or die, and he'd give the Goodwin girl to his son, marriage or not. Daub could not abide by that and reluctantly he agreed, knowing his own chances for leaving this place alive were slim. If he ever did, he swore he'd bring back aid, and rescue the child . . . and a marriage to a dead man is no marriage at all. He recoiled at these thoughts, but his own sense of justice had been pushed over the line sometime during the night as he sat tied to the chair watching Ribalt's pitiful wife melt into a corner each time he entered the house.

In her own way to make something of the marriage, Yellow Leaf knitted together a garland of yellow and gold leaves to place around Sarah Goodwin's neck. She swept out the dirt floor of the cabin and settled the dust with a sprinkle of water.

At noon, Ribalt ordered the wedding party into the yard in front of his cabin. He opened the smokehouse door and brought the terrified girl out into the daylight. Sarah Goodwin looked young and vulnerable, and she viewed the scene before her with wide, frightened eyes that lingered a moment on the bruised and disheveled Reverend Daub, who looked as unhappy about this affair as she.

How she longed for her mother's comforting arms, her father's strength. She hated what she knew was to follow. At fourteen, Sarah Goodwin was no more ready for marriage than she was for dying. And right now, the second choice was infinitely preferable.

"Come here, girl," Ribalt said, taking her by the arm. He stood her next to Jimmy, who grinned and ran his fingers nervously through his stringy hair.

"Ribalt, I plead with you," Daub started to say.

Ribalt stuck his rifle into Daub's ribs. "I don't want to hear your pleading, preacher man. All I want to hear are the proper words to marry up these two young'uns. And I want to hear you start saying them now!"

Sarah began to whimper. Jimmy's grin grew wider. Yellow Leaf draped the garland of leaves over Sarah's head and tied a pretty bow in her smudged calico bonnet. There was a tear of regret in her black eyes. She glanced away so that Ribalt would not see.

Daub looked at the rifle barrel in his ribs, then fumbled open his worn Bible. Every fiber of his being rebelled against this act, but certain death awaited if he disobeyed.

"Get with it, preacher."

Daub cleared his throat and began to recite the wedding ceremony.

THIRTY

BEFORE THE SUN WAS UP, McKendree and Duchess had been on their way for over an hour. It was near noon when he crested a ridge and saw chimney smoke in the clearing beyond. His moccasins made no noise as he threaded his way to the house. The rifle he'd taken from Sculty felt the tension in his hands, and it alone, if it had had consciousness, would have known that McKendree was not merely stalking deer for the pot, but much deadlier game.

Where the trees opened up, McKendree dropped to a crouch and moved behind the barn, eyeing the woodpile there. A misplaced step could give him away. He turned around the corner, and his breathing stopped.

There was the Reverend Daub, and there was Sarah Goodwin, and there was the whole Ribalt family gathered about, too. For an instant McKendree was bewildered, then the wind shifted and he heard the words Daub was reciting.

". . . do you, Sarah Goodwin, take this man—?"

"No! No, no, no," came a tearful reply. The voice of the child that McKendree had held on his knee as a baby, and later had played with his son . . . *Lucas*. A mountain of emotion erupted within him like a volcano. He pushed it down before it had a chance to take hold of him. It was plain now what had happened. The fears Charles Goodwin had revealed to him had come true. He could only guess what had happened to Charles and Rachael. They would never have permitted this.

That meant they were dead. At the very least, it was a thing he had to consider. A study of the scene unfolding in the dusty yard told him that Reverend Daub had not fared well. His clothes had the tattered, dusty look of a pauper, and his face was swollen. Even so, he looked better off than Ribalt's wife. McKendree could not guess what had descended upon the poor woman to so brutally disfigure her face.

His attention went back to Sarah Goodwin, small and pitiful in a dirty dress. Ribalt's gruff voice rang out. "She does, preacher man. Pay no mind to her words."

Daub stopped defiantly and glared at Ribalt. The trapper's rifle jabbed out, buckling Daub over. "You just say the words you're supposed to. Any more trouble, preacher man, and I'll bury you out behind the barn." Ribalt glanced away in that direction and McKendree pulled back a hairsbreadth ahead of him.

One sure thing would end this, he figured, raising his rifle. Then Daub's shoulder came between him and Ribalt. McKendree drew back. There was Sarah to consider too. He'd have to draw the fight away from the house.

McKendree stepped out into the open and said, "Ribalt!"

Ribalt's head came around and his face went rigid. Shock immediately turned to rage. "McKendree! I left you dead back at the river."

"You made a mistake, Ribalt, and it's going to cost you." Suddenly McKendree was gone, and only the quivering of a leaf marked the place where he had stood.

"Jimmy! Antoine! Git your guns!" Ribalt barked.

Yellow Leaf put out a hand to stop Antoine. Ribalt slapped it away. "It's time he grows up, woman."

She released her hold on Antoine and hurried Louis into the house. Ribalt motioned Daub and Sarah into the smokehouse and rammed the iron bar through the door handle.

Hidden in the thick timber, McKendree checked the prime in both his guns. Duchess seemed to know what was to come next.

"Pa, where'd he go?" came Jimmy's voice. McKendree locked onto it like a hawk circling a rodent.

Ribalt said, "Keep bright now, boys. Don't show him your blind side."

"How we supposed to find him?" Antoine said.

"Keep talkin' and he'll find you!" Ribalt rebuked, and after that all McKendree heard was the soft padding of their feet upon the forest floor.

Antoine passed near him with no notion of how close death hovered. McKendree put the boy in his sights, but at the last moment raised the rifle, uncertain why. Antoine was Lucas' age, McKendree realized all at once. He stepped up behind the boy and clipped him over the head with his rifle. He tossed the boy's rifle away and paused to listen.

He picked up their sounds. Duchess stayed near, as if waiting for a cue. McKendree gave none. This was his fight and she had no part in it. Then the forest grew quiet, as if life had suddenly frozen in time. McKendree froze too.

A rifle shot rang out, splintering tree bark stung his cheek. He dove and rolled, coming to his feet and darting off in the opposite direction.

"I hit him, Pa! I hit him!" Jimmy said, but when he reached the place, McKendree was gone.

"Load up, boy," Ribalt ordered, eyeing the deep forest, his rifle swinging this way and that.

McKendree drew up in the shadow of a big white pine and sleeved the blood from his cheek. Duchess' drawn-back lips showed sharp white teeth. "You'd like a piece of him, wouldn't you?" he whispered. If she could speak, he knew what her reply would be.

He moved out, keeping to the shadows, and found the boy skulking along a deer trace, looking constantly to either side. McKendree had lost track of Jacques Ribalt but knew he was nearby. Their cat-and-mousing had carried them far up the hillside. He could have killed the boy right there, but it was Jacques Ribalt he really wanted. He moved up close and stepped out in the open. Jimmy came up short, startled.

"Drop it," McKendree said, and there was no room in his voice for any argument. Jimmy reached back and set his rifle against a tree.

"You gonna kill me?" he asked, beginning to shake some.

"Anything is possible." McKendree turned the boy around and put his rifle to the boy's back. "Ribalt! Jacques Ribalt! I have your son. Show yourself or I'll do him like you did mine."

After a moment, Ribalt emerged from the shadows, as if an instant before, his huge body had had no substance. He held his rifle on McKendree with Jimmy between them. "You just don't know when to die, do you, McKendree? That fall would have killed most men."

"I reckon it wasn't my time, Ribalt."

"Then this will be your time," he said, his mouth a scowl deep within the black, wiry nest of his beard. "Step away from the boy and face me like a man."

"Like a man?" McKendree's laugh was bitter as the cold winds of winter. "Like a man who kills children and beats women. Like a man who sends his Indian brothers out to kill innocent travelers." He was thinking suddenly of George Winfield, and how he had died. "You look with favor on this boy, Ribalt. Unless you want to see him dead, you'll drop that gun."

"So's you can kill me?"

"That's my intention."

Ribalt laughed. "Go to hell, McKendree. And take the boy with you."

"Pa?" Jimmy said, stunned.

"He ain't gonna kill you, boy," Ribalt said confidently.

Out of the corner of his eye, McKendree saw movement. In the next instant Duchess was in motion, her teeth bared, her fur about her neck standing straight. Ribalt saw her too, and as she leaped he swung his rifle and fired. The dog yelped and fell to the ground. McKendree pushed Jimmy Ribalt aside and fired. Ribalt clutched his shoulder, the rifle slipping from his fingers. Then he disappeared into the forest.

Jimmy scrambled to his feet, diving for his rifle against the tree. McKendree was already moving to where the dog lay when he realized what the boy was up to. He fell to the ground, slipping the blunderbuss off his shoulder as he moved. Both weapons exploded at once. A cloud of smoke obscured his vision, and when it cleared, Jimmy Ribalt was dead.

McKendree left the boy and knelt over Duchess. The dog looked up at him with large brown eyes. Her tongue lolled as she panted. "You're bad hurt, girl," he said, putting a hand on her coarse yellow fur, feeling her strong heart beating. There was blood on her chest, and now it had begun to trickle from her mouth. "I appreciate what you tried to do. I reckon it was your fight after all. I reckon you had a score to settle on Duke's account. . . ."

McKendree heard Ribalt suddenly behind him. He rolled instantly to the left as the big man brought a knife down and sliced empty air. McKendree regained his feet and pulled his own knife free. The two men circled. Ribalt was as big as any bear he'd ever faced, and ten times as cunning. He was wounded and enraged. He outweighed McKendree by fifty pounds and topped him a good five inches. The small trickle of blood down his left sleeve told McKendree his bullet had not done the damage he had hoped it had. "You killed my boy!" Ribalt bellowed and lunged.

McKendree's side had begun to ache. His sudden leap rearward to clear the slashing blade brought a spasm of pain. Ribalt struck out again. McKendree judged where the knife was going, swung his leg at it and missed, losing his balance. He caught himself in time to catch Ribalt's wrist as the trapper drove in with what would surely have been the fatal plunge. Ribalt's momentum carried McKendree to the ground, and his knife went flying. Ribalt's wrist was thick as a fence rail. McKendree held it off with both hands as the point of Ribalt's knife danced above his throat.

With Ribalt's massive weight behind it, the knife slowly moved toward McKendree's jugular. McKendree's shoulders and arms bunched, drawing from unknown reserves to keep it back. But he was no match for Ribalt where sheer strength mattered. McKendree lifted his head and sank his teeth into Ribalt's hand.

Crying out, Ribalt instinctively drew back. McKendree drove a knee into the trapper's side and rolled from beneath him, scrambling to his feet. He searched the ground for his knife, instead saw his rifle, and snatched it up, swinging out. It struck Ribalt in the side and the stock snapped clean off at the lock.

Ribalt shook off the blow and came back twice as mad. Blood dripped from teeth marks at Ribalt's wrist, and like a wounded bear, Ribalt plunged ahead heedless of the consequences. The knife drove up. McKendree managed to avoid it, and then his heel snagged and he stumbled backward, catching himself at the last minute. Ribalt was on him at once. McKendree caught the wrist again, but his energy was draining. His breathing seared his lungs, and the wound flared like a firebrand caught beneath his shirt. Locked in a fight to the death, McKendree found himself being forced back toward the trees.

Then he stepped under the knife, turning Ribalt around. They separated for an instant and Ribalt took a step back to steady himself. At that moment, something leaped up like a snake from the forest floor and grabbed hold of Ribalt at mid-leg. Only it had jaws of iron instead of bone. Ribalt let out a cry that was a mix of shock and pain and lost his balance. The spring trap locked, holding him as it had a hundred animals before him. McKendree kicked the knife from his fist and snatched it up.

Ribalt backpedaled until the chain went taut. McKendree moved over him, and for the first time he saw fear in Ribalt's eyes. Trapped, Ribalt was a dead man, and he knew it . . . that was how it should be. McKendree could have had his life now, but he hesitated. He thought of Lucas, buried behind the cabin, and of Ribalt's boy, dead a few feet away. He remembered George Winfield, and all the men who had died back at the cave. The killing had gone on and on, and the man responsible was beneath his knife.

But McKendree couldn't kill like this. No matter how deep the hate ran, he couldn't kill a man who could no longer fight back. The killing had to stop somewhere. Someone had to say, *enough*. With disgust, McKendree heaved the knife away.

"You're letting me live?" Ribalt said in a faltering voice.

"Your son is dead. I'm going to let you bury him, to feel the pain of it right down to the bottom of your black soul." He turned abruptly and strode away.

"McKendree!" Ribalt yelled. "I'll kill you yet!" and he reached for the blade in the top of his moccasin. McKendree turned in time to see the knife in Ribalt's hand, and he saw something else too, something yellow and red moving across the ground in long, fluid strides. Ribalt's attention was turned full on McKendree, and he never saw Duchess leaping for his great bearded throat. With white teeth flashing, she tore the life from the man. There was no scream; there was no time for one. Her teeth brought forth a fountain of blood and Ribalt's heart pumped the life from his body. And then he died. Duchess, panting her last, and having settled the score on Duke's account, died with him.

McKendree stood over the two bodies. The circle had closed.

Ribalt had died even as he had killed. McKendree touched the dead dog sadly, turning a cold, contemptuous eye on Ribalt. He took up the blunderbuss, stopped to view Jimmy's bloody body, then walked down the trace and gathered the unconscious Antoine into his arms.

Yellow Leaf stood back from the door when McKendree stepped inside and put Antoine on the bed. "My husband, and my son?" she asked.

He did not have to say the words for her to know. She saw it in his eyes and nodded her head in acceptance. "Thank you for bringing Antoine back to me."

McKendree removed the iron rod from the smokehouse door. The warm afternoon light shone upon Sarah and Daub. "Let's go home," he said. With a sudden release of emotion, Sarah put her arms around his waist and tears moistened his shirt. He picked her up, carried her to Ribalt's horses and saddled one. Daub said he'd stay with Yellow Leaf awhile.

With Sarah seated behind him, McKendree rode away.

The Great
Western
Wilderness

THIRTY-ONE

"RACHAEL! Rachael, she's back!" Charles Goodwin had seen McKendree and Sarah ride into the yard through the window, and now his feet seemed unable to decide which way to rush. In the end, he shouted the good news to his wife in the bedroom and bolted out the door.

McKendree stopped and lowered Sarah to the ground, where Charles swooped her up into his arms. Tears streamed down both daughter's and father's cheeks. At the doorway, Rachael grasped the door frame for support, looking drawn and pale. McKendree knew full well how worry would do that to a person. Charles carried Sarah to Rachael and she added her arms to the tangle.

McKendree didn't dismount. Goodwin put Sarah into Rachael's care, who seemed to be shedding her illness even as the tears of happiness rolled over her cheeks. "Josh," he said, stopping by the horse, "how did it go?" There was a change in his friend, a somber aloneness he'd seen a time or two in the faces of travelers with no place to call home. "We thought you had . . ." He hesitated. "When your horse returned alone . . . well, we just figured you wouldn't be coming back."

McKendree's face no longer wore its customary easiness, and the eyes that peered down at Charles Goodwin had a hard look in them. "It's a long story, Charles. The short of it is, Ribalt won't be bothering you any longer." He glanced at Sarah, "And Jimmy Ribalt won't be bothering your girl anymore either."

"It was the Ribalts that took her?"

McKendree nodded his head.

"Josh, light down and come into the house."

McKendree drew himself up wearily in the saddle. "I can't. I got to get home. I want to see Noreen."

Charles looked at him, startled, and said, "You haven't been back then?"

"I came here first. Sarah needed you, and I figured you needed her."

"We did, we truly did, Josh," he said, looking at the new surge of vitality he saw in his wife's face. He turned back. "Josh, Noreen . . . well, she didn't make it. She's with Lucas."

McKendree had expected that. He had readied himself for it although he had prayed it would not be so. Now he sat astride the horse, feeling an intense emptiness.

"We did what we could for her, but she never regained consciousness. We're truly sorry, Josh."

McKendree glanced away and rubbed at the corners of his eyes. When he looked back he said, "I know you did, Charles." With no further words, McKendree reined his horse around and rode away.

Back on the porch, Rachael said, "Go with him, Charles. He needs you."

Goodwin shook his head. "No, he'll need us tomorrow. Today, he needs to be alone. I know him. This is something he'll want to work through without me getting in the way."

McKendree dismounted in the yard. It seemed wider than the last time he'd seen it, and dustier. A scattering of fall leaves crunched beneath his feet. The tall corn was yellow, and the horse in the corral seemed well fed. He stepped up on the porch and pushed the door open.

Nothing had changed. If he had tried, he could have imagined Noreen standing in the corner polishing the mirror as she had done every Wednesday of their married life. He glanced around the cabin —Lucas' bedding up in the loft, the table he'd build that first year, the stove he and Noreen's father had hauled down by wagon from St. Louis—everywhere he looked, he saw his family. This was their home as well as his, and forever their memory would remain here. It was not a place for him anymore.

Out back he brushed the fall leaves from the two fresh graves and stared at the carefully made crosses that marked them.

Memorials.

Lucas hadn't needed them to remember, and McKendree figured he didn't either. For always, Noreen and Lucas would be alive in his memory. Like Carlotta's Indian jewels; *All you got to do is get them wet again. They will always be . . . magical.* He touched his pocket, felt the stones and remembered. He needed something, he thought, something that had been important to both of them.

Back inside, the quietness reminded him of a church. In the corner was the stick Lucas used to pretend was a rifle, and beside it the shiny new gun McKendree had brought for him that day. . . . It would have been the most valued possession Lucas had. McKendree set it on the table and glanced about, knowing exactly what he was looking for. He found the Bible on the floor by Noreen's side of the bed. He opened her Bible to the front where she had meticulously recorded the family's records—births, marriages . . . deaths. Fetching ink and quill, he carefully completed the history, blotted the ink dry and put the Bible into his saddlebags.

Evening was coming on when McKendree carried the rifle and saddlebags to the barn, setting the blunderbuss and hunting bag with them. Other than shot and powder, he took nothing else. He put Ribalt's horse into the corral with his own and grained the animals, then he took one last walk around the property, coming finally back to the graves. In the dark, he stood over them, until the chill fall air drove him into the house for his heavy coat. He shrugged into it and buttoned it closed. There was nothing left to do now, and retrieving a can of coal oil from behind the cabin, he went around the cabin dousing the walls. He poured the rest of it inside, on the table and the bed, and struck a lucifer against the door post.

The funeral pyre consumed what had been his life, and all that he had loved. He stood in the yard throughout the night as the flames licked skyward and then in slow degrees died down to bright embers that lit McKendree's somber face where he stood, staring. A morning fog came across the land before dawn, chilled and damp. McKendree remained huddled in his heavy coat watching his home return to the land from where he had fashioned it.

With the dawn, the fog burned off. The cabin was mostly a heap of gray ash with only a corner of the log wall and the stone chimney still standing. McKendree saddled his horse and rode away, refusing to give it even a backward glance.

He reined to a stop in front of the Goodwins' cabin. Charles stepped out, hitching a suspender strap over his shoulder.

"Josh, are you all right?"

McKendree nodded his head. "I'm going to be fine. It's just going to take some time."

"We saw the night sky aglow. I wanted to come but figured you needed to be alone."

He said, "I'm leaving."

Rachael stepped out beside her husband. "Where will you go, Josh?"

"I haven't quite made up my mind. West, I figure. There's a lot of country out that way to be seen, and besides, I sort of made someone a promise." He fished the newspaper clipping from his pocket, tattered and dog-eared, and handed it down to Charles.

"The Great Western Wilderness?" Goodwin said, raising a quizzical eye, handing the paper back to him.

"It's a start," he said.

"I think I understand," Rachael said. "Will we ever see you again?"

"I don't know," he said truthfully. "I want to thank you for your friendship, and the way you looked after the place and all. You can have my livestock, Charles, and whatever you manage to harvest from the fields. You can take the land too, if you like. It's yours. The horse in the corral belongs to Yellow Leaf. I'd appreciate it if you see she gets it back."

"I will," Goodwin said, "but I won't take your land. I'll watch over it and work it, but when you come back, it'll be waiting for you."

McKendree nodded his head. "That sounds fair enough. Well, goodbye then." He stretched out a hand, then turned his horse away.

Rachael said suddenly, "Wait a minute, Josh," and she hurried back into the house. When she came back out a feisty puppy squirmed in her hands. A big yellow puppy that was a ringer for

Duke and Duchess. "Noreen wanted this one. She thought it looked like Duke. Here, you take it."

"I don't know—"

"Please, Josh," she said. "After all, a man ain't properly outfitted for the frontier if he ain't got a dog." She handed it up to him.

McKendree held it up. The puppy tried to lick his nose. "She's grown some, hasn't she?" he said, grinning.

"Noreen wanted to name him Little Duke. She'd want you to have her."

"Well, I guess if Noreen would want it, it must be the right thing to do." McKendree settled the puppy across the front of his saddle. "Thank you."

"You take care, now. And come back sometime," Charles said.

"We'll see," McKendree said, and with that he turned his horse away. Where life would take him now, he did not know. He'd start in Independence, and see what Colonel William T. MacNamarra had to offer, and he'd take a gander at that "Great Western Wilderness" for Winfield's sake, and then . . .

Well, who knows, he thought, as he rode away from there, toward a new life.

ABOUT THE AUTHOR

Douglas Hirt lives in Colorado, at the base of Pikes Peak, with his wife, Kathy, and their two children, Rebecca and Derick. His previous Double D Westerns are *Devil's Wind* and *A Passage of Seasons*.